The Wrong Way to Use Healing Magic

1

KUROKATA

ONE PEACE BOOKS

Usato

Rose

Character Introductions

That was when something struck me as odd.
I was knee-deep in an ocean of the enemy's blood.
It seemed that I had wiped out
all the kingdom's knights in the area.
Slaughtering them was so easy
that I didn't realize
I'd done it.

"What a bore," I said.

"Humans are
too easy to kill."

CONTENTS

Rescue Team Guidelines
Stance on the battlefield

Prioritize saving lives at all costs.
Protect the lives of friends and foes alike.
Punch the martyrs who want to die
and drag them off the battlefield.

PROLOGUE

It was a dismal rainy day.

Raindrops pattered loudly against the ground as they descended from the sky. I stared vacantly at the crowded entrance, annoyed by the relentless sound of the rain.

The downpour had suddenly started in the afternoon. I didn't have an umbrella on me—especially after forgetting to check the weather that morning—but I did keep a foldable umbrella at school in case of sudden rainy days like today. I walked over to the umbrella stand to go get it.

"It's gone," I stated flatly.

It was supposed to be there, but it wasn't. Somebody probably took it. My conspicuous black umbrella was there in the morning, but it had seemingly vanished.

"Just my luck," I grumbled.

I probably should've been angry, but I wasn't in the slightest. I simply stood there slowly looking up at the raindrops that continued to fall from the roof of the school's entryway. I don't know whether it was the dampness in the air or the feeling that night was approaching, but for some reason that rainy day made me want to reexamine my life.

"School again tomorrow. Sure wish we had the day off," I mumbled under my breath.

I was a regular student at school. I had my fair share of friends, decent grades, and I wasn't too bad at sports. If someone asked me to list my strengths and weaknesses, nothing would come to mind right away, and I didn't have any hobbies to speak of.

My name's Ken Usato. Unlike my last name, Usato, which is admittedly pretty unusual, my existence can be summed up by my first name: Ken, the blandest name in existence. Everyone—including me—knows I'm nothing special.

I'm ordinary and I'm okay with it, but I was still far from satisfied with my life. Nothing was holding me back in particular, so I doubted that anyone would understand why I was so discontented. I was unsatisfied on a more fundamental level. The problem was that . . .

I've always admired the supernatural—the faraway world of fantasy.

I wanted drastic changes that would shake up my everyday life. It didn't matter how it happened. I just wanted to break away from the status quo and do something that was different from the norm—to bid farewell to the ordinary Usato, who could only respond with a wry smile when people said that I was unremarkable, but still "such a nice guy."

Sigh.

But opportunities like that don't come around every day. I couldn't escape my reality, and worlds of fiction and fantasy were far out of my reach.

People don't change as easily as they do in manga or anime. They never change unless a dramatic event changes the course of their lives, and I was no different. I was doomed to take that ordinary life to my grave, whereas the perfect world in my head was anything but realistic.

But no matter how much I whined about life, reality wasn't going to change. I was ordinary through and through, so I had completely given up hope.

"What am I thinking?" I asked myself.

Was I that far down the rabbit hole? How embarrassing.

I leaned back against the wall of the school's entryway and sighed. Most of the students had already gone home. My breathing and the heavy rain were the only sounds I could hear.

"Guess I'll stay here for a while. Don't wanna get wet," I whispered.

I stood alone at the school's entryway and kept watching the rain. There was no rush to go home, so I wasn't going to force myself to brave the harsh weather.

"How is it still raining?!" I asked, still talking to myself.

Even after an hour of waiting, the rain showed no sign of stopping.

It was just past 5:30 p.m. and students from various clubs

had started packing up to go home. At this rate, it seemed that I had no choice but to head out in the dark and return home soaking wet.

I contemplated "borrowing" one of the items that were left in the umbrella stand, but I ultimately decided against it. I didn't want the guilt and the trouble that would inevitably come with that decision. As fed up as I was, I was too chicken to do it and decided to wait a bit longer.

"If it gets any darker, I'll . . . huh?" I faltered.

I was standing there alone when two students—a male and a female—appeared in the school's entryway. The most succinct way to describe them would be to call them a "good-looking pair."

The boy was Kazuki Ryusen—a classmate of mine. His name looked cool in katakana, but it was even cooler in kanji. He was tall and handsome and pretty close to perfect. A popular protagonist-type whose looks could put any virtual boyfriend to shame. His good looks and personality mesmerized all the girls at school.

Not only that, but he was also the vice president of the student council. He was an almost supernatural being whose backstory couldn't be any more perfect. Honestly, I've always wanted to see him randomly blow up in class.

Oh shit, he's looking right at me.

"Hey," the girl said.

"What's wrong, Inukami-senpai?" Ryusen responded.

"He . . ."

Suzune Inukami was the one who'd noticed me. She was an upperclassman in her third year, and the current president of the student council—a beautiful girl whose black hair framed her dignified face. She was a star pupil and athlete whose wit and beauty would make any fictional character blush. All the boys admired her. She even remained popular among the uppity girls on the student council.

Honestly, she was way out of my league. Not that it mattered, though, since I'd heard rumors that she and Ryusen were dating. In any case, she had seen me standing despondently by the shoe cubbies. Together they approached me.

"You don't have an umbrella?" she asked.

"Um, well . . . no, I don't," I responded.

"I see. I guess you were waiting for the rain to let up, huh? Looks like school's about to close."

Is it that late already?

I peered outside as I checked the time on my cell phone. I considered asking my parents to pick me up, but I knew they couldn't make it since they both had to work. After telling Inukami about my predicament, she frowned and crossed her arms.

"Sending a student home sopping wet would sully the student council's reputation," she stated.

"Senpai, I'll lend him my umbrella," Ryusen said.

He told me that it was foldable and then kindly handed it over. Now I understood. All the girls liked him because he was genuinely nice.

This was my first time talking to him since we became classmates. Despite this, simply talking to him felt like a breath of fresh air. I was also kind of touched that he happened to remember my name.

"Thanks, Ryusen-kun."

"Hey, we're in the same class, aren't we? Calling me by my last name is, I don't know, too formal. You can call me Kazuki. Should I call you Usato? Or Ken?"

"Usato works."

There were already so many Kens at school and we didn't need another. Besides, I was personally a fan of the name Usato and would much rather be called that over "Ken."

But really, I never thought I'd see the day when the coolest guy in school would know my name! That basically means we're already friends! All the girls are gonna look at me with hearts (daggers) in their eyes tomorrow when they see us together.

"Does that mean I can call you Usato-kun too?" asked Inukami.

"Uh . . . s-sure!"

It wasn't only the girls, now I also had to worry about the envious stares from all the guys at school. The most beautiful girl in school was calling me by my name! I could die a happy man.

Man, here I was thinking what a rotten day this was but it's actually the opposite. Now I'm friends with the most popular students in school! A real once in a lifetime opportunity. Rain is the best. I say keep it coming!

I was busy apologizing in my head to the rain.

"Well then, what do you say we head home?" said Kazuki. He invited me to tag along.

Kazuki seemed a little more excited than normal, possibly because we'd just become friends. At first, I was worried that he liked me in **that** kind of way, but I soon realized that he was simply happy to have another guy to hang out with. I cursed myself for having doubted him and apologized to him in my head.

Inukami didn't seem to mind that I was there, so we all left school together.

"Have you thought about what you want to do after you graduate, Usato-kun?" Inukami asked abruptly.

I gave her a vague answer. "Not really, I'm only a second-year after all."

"You asked me the same thing the other day, senpai," Kazuki noted.

"Heh. That's because I don't have any plans. I can't help but wonder what other people want to do."

The sounds of rushing rain and our footsteps echoed around us. I thought about how peaceful it sounded.

Talking to them felt strangely reassuring. Were those two

giving off real-life good vibes? Talking to my friends felt totally different. My friends were always so insufferable, yet I felt somewhat refreshed talking to Inukami and Kazuki.

As I basked in that feeling, I decided to ask Inukami a question.

"Do you know what you want to do after you graduate? Since you're a third-year and all."

"Nope."

"Aren't you cutting it kinda close?"

It might have been rude, but it was honestly what I was thinking. Inukami was already a third-year and graduation wasn't far off.

She smiled wryly in response. There was something very masochistic about it. The smile didn't look right, especially not on the distinguished face of the student president who was idolized by all the students.

"Yeah, but I don't know what I want to do with my life. Once I set a goal, I achieve it immediately. It makes me feel like I don't belong here or something."

"You're so talented, senpai," I marveled.

"Seriously," said Kazuki.

The impression I had of her was that she can play sports and study hard—that she could do anything. Yet here she was worried about something that I never worried about. The things we worried about may have been different, but I was sure we were both worried about *something*, nonetheless.

"Oh, I didn't mean for that to come off as arrogant or anything," she quickly interjected.

Kazuki and I looked at each other and smiled, as if to say, "Don't worry, we know."

Inukami's cheeks turned bright red. She turned away as if she was angry at something.

"By the way, is it true that you two are . . . dating?" I asked.

"What? Um, no. Me . . . with senpai? No way," answered Kazuki.

"What he said. People often mistake us for a couple, but that's only because we work together for the student council."

Wait, really?

As someone who also thought they were dating, I was speechless.

"You're kidding," I said.

"Why would I joke about that? Senpai and I are just friends." He smiled wryly.

I stared at him with a dumbfounded expression.

The rumor was totally false.

But the truth was that Kazuki was much friendlier than I'd ever thought. He would make the same uneasy, wry smile whenever he talked to a girl from our class. My friends and I used to glare and call him a stupid normie because we were jealous, but I didn't see him that way anymore.

I told him that I used to think he was hard to approach.

"Looks who's talking," he said, flashing another wry smile.

I only talked to a few friends at school, so maybe I really was hard to approach. Still, knowing that people thought that didn't make me feel good. We kept walking, talking about whatever was on our minds, when suddenly Kazuki and Inukami froze in place.

I stopped a step later and turned around to see what was happening. They were both cupping their ears with their hands as if they were trying to hear something more clearly.

"Hey, what's wrong?" I asked.

"Usato, did you hear that just now? There was a ringing sound," Kazuki asked me.

"I didn't hear it," I said.

"I heard it too. Was that . . . the sound of a bell?" asked Inukami.

But there were no buildings around us that had any bells.

I was the only one who couldn't hear it. I felt a little left out.

"Are you okay?" I started to take a step toward them. I was curious as to what might have happened.

But the moment I took a step toward them, geometrical shapes suddenly floated up to our feet—no, to the concrete below us. Working at the speed of light, the few gray cells I had in my gamer brain translated these shapes into words.

"Is this . . . a magic circle?" I inquired.

There's no way that magic circles exist. Not in a world where science rules!

I watched the situation unfold around me. I was so panicked that it actually had the opposite effect, and I began to feel calm. The light from the magic circle on the ground flickered.

Leaving an ordinary world.

Switching to fantasy.

Walking a different path in life.

Starting a heart-pounding adventure.

These thoughts spun around in my head.

"Kazuki! W-What do you think of other worlds?" I shouted.

"What? What're you talking about, Usato?! And what's going on? Is this a prank show or something?!"

Crap. It was too early for him to understand what I'd meant.

I felt optimistic, at first. But seeing Kazuki panic made me realize the gravity of the situation.

"Usato! Do other worlds have magic and monsters . . . and heroes?!" Inukami shouted with a calm smile on her face.

Inukami is surprisingly nerdy, like me!

She must read light novels.

I heard they're dirty!

Feeling calmed by her words, I responded.

"I feel like you and I are going to be really good friends, Inukami!"

While all this was happening, the magic circle shone so bright it was blinding.

I closed my eyes at the overwhelming light and started feeling nauseous and dizzy. Then I lost consciousness.

CHAPTER 1

Dragged into Another World!

Halfway conscious, I felt the cold floor beneath me. I opened my eyes.

"Huh? Where am I?" I whispered.

I found myself in a spacious, luxurious hall.

There was a bearded man sitting in a large chair in front of me, surrounded by a good number of elderly men. It was impossible to comprehend what was going on since I was still half-conscious. When I focused a little more on the bearded man, I realized that he was sitting on some sort of throne. He was clad in lavish, foreign clothes and wearing a crown.

The old men behind him are dressed like royal attendants from my RPGs!

As my eyes shifted from the old men to my other surroundings, a group of different men came into view. Adorned in armor and Western-looking swords, the men appeared to be soldiers standing in a line side by side.

"Hey. Are you okay, Usato?" asked Kazuki. He was seated next to me and had an apprehensive look in his eyes.

Thank goodness the three of us didn't get separated. If Kazuki's here, that probably means that senpai's close by.

"Kazuki . . . what happened?" I asked, surveying the room. I discovered that Inukami was sitting beside me and had already waken up.

Sleepy-eyed senpai is so sexy!

I was merely avoiding reality by filling my head with pervy thoughts.

"I'm not sure. All I know is that when I woke up, I was surrounded by people who were wearing weird clothes."

"Gotcha. Are you okay, senpai?"

"Oh, no need to worry. I am completely unharmed."

The man in the crown noticed that we were awake and was staring right at us. His solemn gaze was a little intimidating.

"It appears they have awoken," he said.

The man looked incredibly important, so I couldn't imagine what he could have wanted from students like us. With my head still in a daze, I slowly looked around the room to get a grasp on the situation. Kazuki cautiously turned to the man in the crown.

"Who the hell're all of you?" Kazuki said.

The kingly figure's guards weren't pleased with his presumptuous tone. "You cur! How dare you disrespect His Majesty!" they shouted. But the kingly figure quieted his attendants with a wave of his hand.

"No matter. Saying such things is only natural when you suddenly find yourself in a place like this. Do not look down on them, Sergio."

"B-But . . . understood," Sergio replied.

"Pardon him. He is quite stubborn," remarked the crowned figure.

"Y-Yes, your majesty . . ." Sergio admitted.

"My name is Lloyd Vulgast Llinger, king of Llinger Kingdom."

Llinger Kingdom . . . nope, never heard of that country before. Not that I know the name of every country in the world, anyway.

"Allow me to speak frankly. You have been summoned to Llinger Kingdom to serve as our heroes," said the king.

"Did you just say *heroes*?" asked Kazuki in disbelief.

Just then, I heard someone next to me whisper "I knew it!"

I'm just gonna believe senpai didn't say that just now. Senpai, please don't destroy your image as a cold-hearted queen any more than you already have! Kazuki's being serious, so calm yourself down!

"Indeed. In this world, the Demon Lord, the being who reigns supreme over all demons, has been resurrected. He commands an army that is quickly recruiting soldiers across the land. Two years ago, the people of Llinger Kingdom took part in a battle that they knew would likely cost them their lives. Although we fought with great vigor, we barely survived against the Demon Lord's powerful forces."

"D-Demon Lord?" Kazuki stammered.

"At the end of that frantic struggle, we somehow managed to drive their forces away. However, there is no telling when they might strike next. Therefore, we had no choice but to turn to our last resort—to use forbidden techniques and summon otherworldly beings capable of vanquishing the Demon Lord."

Senpai, I know you're hyped, but now's not the time to be happily slapping your legs! My image of you is crumbling—no, it's crumbled. Now it's just a pile of dust.

"We're 'capable'?" Inukami muttered.

"The magic circle summons those who are capable of being heroes and transports them to our world. When you were being summoned, did you not hear the sound of a bell?"

"So that's what that sound was. But that means Usato—" Kazuki turned to me. He looked like he felt sorry for me.

It was a ringing sound that only those who are capable can hear. In other words, I couldn't hear it, so I wasn't capable.

"Was I . . . brought here by accident?" I inquired.

It was the only reasonable conclusion.

It's okay, guys. I don't mind! Plus, I've got plenty of redeeming qualities. I reaaally hate losing and I'll never give up!

Inukami and Kazuki stared at me with perplexed looks on their faces. From that alone, I could tell that I didn't belong in this world. Knowing that I was sent here by accident felt like it was going to shatter my heart. The king noticed that I was holding my chest in pain and gravely closed his eyes.

Oh no. They're gonna get rid of me because I can't help them, aren't they? Why am I the only one who has to play on hard mode?!

"Indeed, you were caught up in the summoning," the king said. "As much as we would like to send you home, an otherworldly summoning is a one-way operation. We can bring outsiders here, but we cannot send them back. That goes for you two as well."

Hey, this king seems pretty nice. Actually, never mind. Hero summoning or not, I can't rush to conclusions about a guy who selfishly drags heroes into his own mess.

But I began to tell him that there were no hard feelings, anyway. "Don't worry ab—"

"This is bullshit!" shouted Kazuki, cutting me off. In response to Kazuki's anger, the soldiers reached for the swords on their hips.

H-Hold up! I get that you're angry, Kazuki, but keep it cool, will ya?! Don't provoke the soldiers unless you wanna get killed!

Kazuki continued. "What's supposed to happen to us?! I've got a family back home! And so does senpai and Usato!"

"I truly am sorry," the king said solemnly, "but we were desperate."

Kazuki clenched his fist and took a step toward the king. We had just become friends, but I began to see what a great guy Kazuki was. Here he was fighting for us, and there I was, such a screwball that I couldn't even get serious.

"Calm down, Kazuki," I said. "Lashing out won't help us."

"Hmph. If you say so, Usato."

My words seemed to affect him more than I'd thought.

The king stood up, then descended from his throne and approached us. He bowed deeply, remorsefully. "I understand it was selfish, but I promise you that I will find a way to send you back home. Until then, I beg you . . . please lend us your power."

As this bizarre scene played out, Kazuki quickly calmed down. He heaved a hopeless sigh and bowed to the king. "I apologize for the outburst. Please tell us everything. We'll take it from there."

"We are grateful for your forgiveness," said the king.

Kazuki turned to me and Inukami and nodded. Giving a thumbs up, Inukami flashed a smile that was more invigorated than I'd ever seen her at school. She was definitely having the most fun out of all of us.

* * *

In the end, Kazuki accepted the king's mission.

Kazuki was originally going to refuse, but he reluctantly accepted when he heard of the terrible conditions that were brought on by the Demon Lord's resurrection. Inukami didn't particularly object to his decision either. Actually, it felt like she was more than ready to go . . . though I had no idea why. As for me? I said that I'd let Kazuki decide—partly because this was entertaining, and partly because they were the only reason I was here in the first place.

A kingdom mage named Welcie had led us out of the grand hall into an old, musty room.

"Now then, Kazuki-sama, Suzune-sama, Usato-sama," said Welcie, "we would like to measure your magical aptitude with this crystal ball."

According to Welcie, simply touching the crystal ball enshrined at the center of the room would show us our "aptitude." In other words, it would tell us what type of magic we'd wield. Apparently, there were many types of magic, with the most traditional being fire, water, lightning, and the like. But there were many other types too, such as teleportation and illusion magic, which only certain races had the ability to use.

I had a hard time believing all this was real. However, I thought that if I could really use magic, I'd want magic that would help me support Inukami and Kazuki. I tested my luck and asked if Welcie could measure my aptitude, too. Even though she instantly approved my request, I knew I'd be super nervous to see what would happen.

"All right, Kazuki-sama, please touch the crystal ball," said Welcie.

I was daydreaming, wondering what ability I'd get as I waited in line, when suddenly I heard Welcie yelp in excitement. I quickly glanced at the crystal ball. It was giving off a white glow under Kazuki's hand.

"Well, if it isn't a true sign of a hero!" Welcie said joyfully.

All this hero stuff makes me feel so left out! Every time I hear the word "hero" my brain feels like a wet tissue that's about to be ripped. Wait, what's this? Kazuki doesn't seem too thrilled.

"What's wrong, Kazuki?" I asked.

"I mean, light? What's so good about that? Do I fight enemies by shining a light in their eyes? What's the point?" he lamented.

"Just shoot 'em with your laser beam, Kazuki-kun!" Inukami exclaimed. "Or use a lightsaber to—"

"Senpai, you shouldn't joke around like that," I said.

This girl is nuts. Bring her to another world and she becomes a total weirdo.

"You're so mean, Usato-kun! But ya know . . . I kinda like it," Inukami said.

Okay, that's just plain creepy. Whoever said she's the prettiest girl in school must be crazy! Oh, wait. That was me.

"No, no, no, you don't understand! Light magic is incredible!" said Welcie. "A truly rare affinity that can only be used by very few people. It boasts unrivaled power in demon battles— the greatest attribute of all!"

"O-Oh, I see," said Kazuki, feeling slightly weirded out by Welcie's enthusiastic explanation. Unable to watch Kazuki any longer, Inukami butted in.

"Can you check what kind of magic I can use next, Welcie?"

"Oh, yes. Certainly. Now then. Please touch the crystal ball like Kazuki-sama did."

Inukami placed her hand on the crystal ball just as Welcie had said.

"Suzune-sama is yellow, meaning that you have an aptitude for lightning magic! You can store just as much magic power as Kazuki-sama!"

"Lightning, huh? Heh heh heh . . ."

So long as senpai's happy, that's all that counts. But even so, lightning? What an affinity. One that every boy admires at least once in their life.

Then the time came—I was up next. I felt a little excited as I drew near the crystal ball, wondering what kind of magic I could possibly use.

"All right, Usato-sama. Please hold out your hand," Welcie said.

"Okay."

I nervously placed my hand on the crystal ball and waited to see what would happen. After a few seconds, the crystal ball turned a slightly transparent shade of green. It was certainly clearer than Kazuki and Inukami's, but the color looked nothing like theirs. It was a color that was easy on the eyes.

Welcie suddenly let out another yelp.

"Um, Welcie?" I stuttered.

Why is she examining the crystal ball up close?

Inukami and Kazuki were also staring at the crystal ball.

"What a beautiful color. It's almost like an emerald green," remarked Inukami.

"Yeah. Mine didn't even have a color—just a flash of light and that's it," added Kazuki.

Welcie had told us that the clearness represents the depth of one's magic power and that the color represents their affinity.

It's kinda clear, so I think it's pretty good? Maybe?

"Does it mean that you control plants? Hey, wait. Is something wrong, Welcie? You're white as a ghost."

"M-Must . . . tell them . . ."

"Pardon?"

Why did Welcie grab my hand?!

"I must tell themmmmm!!!"

She ran out of the room, keeping an iron grip on my hand.

Uh, why? What happened? Did I do something wrong?

We ran back to the great hall where the king was seated. Welcie dragged me before him as I struggled to catch my breath. I hadn't held hands with a girl since the first grade, but this felt somewhat different. If I'm not mistaken, holding hands isn't supposed to involve running full speed out of fear.

"Your Majesty!"

"What is the matter, Welcie? Have you learned their aptitudes? My word, is that Usato? Where are the others?"

"Kazuki-sama and Suzune-sama have incredible potential. It's just that . . ."

"So? Just because Usato was sent here by accident does not mean we shall ignore his wishes."

This guy's too nice to be king.

"It's not that, your majesty! I am fully aware of that. It's his aptitude. It's . . ."

"Whatever could it be? Don't tell me he has the power to control darkness, now does he? Yeah right!" bellowed the king. The king and his men broke out in laughter, but Welcie didn't smile at all. The serious look on her face made me even more nervous.

"The boy . . . is a healer."

"What?! What did you say?"

The laughter suddenly stopped.

"The crystal ball turned green, meaning that he is capable of using healing magic."

Healing . . . magic? What, so I can cure people? That's it?

Silence filled the room.

Why is everyone so quiet? Wait . . . is this m-magic really weak?! Is it so bad that it's not even funny?! I have the power to treat injuries, right? Then why does it feel like we're at a funeral?!

The king looked at me and cleared his throat.

"Having an aptitude for healing magic is unheard of. The ordinary mage can administer basic first aid, but there are very few healers in this country who can heal deeper wounds," said the king with a mix of glee and bewilderment.

"Is that a bad thing?"

"N-No, not at all! You see it's, um . . . w-well, why don't you go to the infirmary in the castle town tomorrow?"

I knew this would happen! Now I'm just scared. What are these people hiding from me?

"You really should, Sir Usato!" The people around me chimed in to agree. "Indeed!"

"What a wonderful development. You simply must go to the infirmary, Usato-sama!"

Welcie's hand started sweating, and it was getting worse by the second.

All of them sounded desperate. It was almost as if they were begging me to go.

"Wait, I thought you said there were other mages who could heal in the kingdom?" I said.

"Listen, those two are fine but **that woman** is no good! No good at all!" the king replied.

Who is this "woman"? And why is the king so afraid of her?

Everyone was nodding profusely, which made it clear that "this woman" was a force to be reckoned with. The moment I opened my mouth to tell the king I would go, a panicked soldier burst through the doorway into the great hall.

"Your Majesty! It's Rose-sama! She's here!"

"What?! Do not let her in the building! Especially not now!" the king said.

"Huh?! But . . ."

Wait. Who the heck is Rose?

The moment I heard her name, the men around begged me

to hide, and to do it at once. I didn't know if hiding would help me, but in any case, I couldn't go anywhere because Welcie was still holding my hand.

You can let go of my hand now, Welcie . . . huh? Did you just say "I'm sorry"? Why are you apologizing to me?

I tried tearing free from Welcie's hand as tears welled up in her eyes. Amid that struggle, the door to the great hall swung open.

"Your Majesty. No one told me the heroes were here."

"Oh no . . ."

Welcie covered her mouth and quietly whispered, "she's here."

A beautiful green-haired woman entered the room. She may have been wearing a thick white robe that looked like a doctor's coat, but the scar that sealed her right eye shut made it clear she was dangerous. She walked straight up to the throne and approached the king, who was now drenched in sweat.

"Why are you so surprised to see me? There somethin' you don't want me to know?"

"Of c-course not, Rose! Didn't you take today off?"

The woman named Rose started glaring at me.

Ack. Who is this scary person? They don't want her to know that I have an aptitude for healing, do they?

"Th-This boy is not a hero! As sad as it may be, our recklessness brought him here by mistake, the poor lad!" the king said frantically.

"You don't say. Boy, what's your name?"

"U-Usato."

"Usato, eh? I'm Rose. Captain of the kingdom's rescue team. At your service."

Rescue . . . team? She saves lives? Looks more like she takes them!

I felt a droplet of sweat run down my face.

"Yes, yes, yes. Now you've met. Usato is quite tired so he should get some rest."

"Makes sense. So, where're the other heroes, Your Majesty?" she demanded.

"Oh, they're right over—"

"Hey! Usato! Are you okay?!" Inukami asked.

Kazuki and Inukami had followed us into the room.

"You just took off, Welcie!" Kazuki announced.

The king glanced over at the two of them.

"There. There are the heroes."

"Oh, nice and fearless, aren't they?" Rose said.

Rose's attention shifted to Kazuki and Inukami. The king was clearly relieved. I couldn't blame him—I was also relieved to have escaped her piercing gaze.

"I'm okay, Kazuki." I said.

"Whew, what was that all about? I don't know what got into you, Welcie, but you really scared us back there. Especially after you looked all scared and dragged Usato out of the room when he made the crystal ball turn green."

Crap. He said it.

At that moment I knew I was done for. I was once again hit with her piercing gaze.

"Did you just say . . . green?" Rose's lips twisted into a smile.

The king looked as if he'd seen a ghost, and of course I looked the same. I was in grave danger for the first time in my life. Kazuki, the perpetrator of this crime, was standing close by. I know he didn't mean to do it, but still . . . I wish he would've realized what was going on, at least.

Rose glared at me as my legs trembled with fear. She was eerily grinning as if I were her prey. She then turned to the king.

"All right, King Lloyd. I'm gonna borrow this runt for a while."

"Welcie! Bring Usato to safety! He is an incredibly important guest in our country! Do not let her take him to that place!" the king ordered.

"To that place? You don't mean . . ." Welcie began.

Welcie jumped out in front of me, wielding a staff. I hid behind her so I couldn't see what was going on. When I moved to the side for visibility, Rose was already gone. Even Welcie uttered a bewildered, "W-Where are you?!"

Suddenly, I felt like I was floating. I was being held in someone's arms! When I looked up, I saw that Rose was carrying me across the floor. I weighed a whole sixty kilograms and yet here she was, carrying me in one arm like it was nothing!

"Your Majesty, I'm gonna turn this kid into a proper healer and don't you forget it!"

The king quickly stood up from his seat. "Wait! I beg you! I know you need a healer, but this boy was merely brought here by chance!" he shouted. But Rose was laughing too hard to hear the king's plea. I had no idea what to do. Kazuki and Inukami looked just as perplexed.

Huh? What is this, a kidnapping?!

When I finally understood what was happening, it was too late. All I could do was avoid meeting the eyes of this woman who savagely smiled at me.

* * *

Usato-kun was taken away.

I calmed myself down for a moment, then turned my attention to King Lloyd.

"But Usato is an average guy who has nothing to do with this!" shouted Kazuki.

I also chimed in. "Where is Usato-kun going? And what did she mean when she said she's going to 'turn him into a healer'?"

Even if I wanted to run away and save him, it was sure to fail. First, I had to get all the information I could out of King Lloyd.

"Welcie, please explain the situation," said King Lloyd, falling back into his seat with a *thud*. He was too exhausted to explain anything himself, so he asked her to do so in his place. This Rose lady must have really worn the king down.

"Yes, your majesty. Umm, you see . . ." started Welcie, taking a few steps toward us, "she is taking him to a place that houses the rescue team—not too far from here. It is managed by Captain Rose, along with her five assistants and two healers. The eight of them run the organization."

"Are there only eight of them? Does that mean they're shorthanded?"

Doesn't it take a much bigger party to fight actual monsters?

"They have enough. Mages can use basic first aid, regardless of aptitude. Therefore, they can heal their own wounds and those of their allies. But graver injuries cannot be healed so quickly. In those cases, we need mages who have the same aptitude as Usato."

So their real ability is to heal people who can't heal them themselves, meaning that Usato-kun may be a very important healer to the kingdom.

"Why didn't you want Rose to look after Usato-kun?"

"May I, Your Majesty?" asked Welcie.

"You may," he said.

Seems pretty complicated.

"Rose-sama is a healing expert. It's just, oh, how do I put it . . . the way she educates her subordinates is a little . . . eccentric."

"Eccentric? In what way?" I asked.

"Well, I don't know too many details, but I hear that she is quite strict. She tells her trainees that being in the rescue team means that they will have to stare death in the face, so she gives them grueling exercises that she claims will teach them techniques to survive the impossible. Most cannot handle such taxing training, so trainees are constantly running away. Originally, the kingdom's knights and the rescue team were supposed to undergo Rose-sama's training together, but the knights couldn't endure it. Now only the rescue team trains under Rose-sama."

"Your knights couldn't take it? Is this Rose person freakishly strong?" I inquired.

King Lloyd rubbed his chin as if he were reliving a fond memory.

"Oh," he answered, "she may be with the rescue team now, but before that she . . . well, we can talk about this later. In any case, the average knight is no match for Rose. When the Demon Lord's army invaded, the rescue team saved a great number of lives. In fact, we couldn't have staved them off without her assistance. As her successes confirm, her training methods are not mistaken. However . . ."

"Yes?" I asked.

Lloyd heaved a heavy sigh, staring into the distance.

"Completing that training comes at a price."

The king clearly couldn't catch a break, and I couldn't help worrying about Usato-kun's safety.

* * *

Rose brought me to a brick house that wasn't too far from the castle.

By that time, the sky had already turned dark.

I entered the building at Rose's request; it was pristine inside. Further into the house were hospital beds and things that I could have only imagined were medical supplies. I surveyed the room as I quietly marveled at how clean it was, and how much it resembled an infirmary.

"This is where you'll live from now on," Rose said.

"Huh?"

"Hey, guys! Say hi to the new kid! Come here!" Rose shouted.

At that moment, I heard footsteps run toward me from the back of the house. The first person who entered the room was a burly man. He stood up straight before Rose.

Um, what? This guy's terrifying!

"Welcome home, Sister Rose!"

"Yo, Alec. Any messages while I was gone?"

"No messages as usual!"

"Oh, good."

Men filled the room behind Alec. I grimaced as I looked at their faces.

Is this yet another world?

"I'm gonna be lookin' after Usato from now on. So play nice with him, got it?"

"Yes, ma'am!" they shouted.

"Great!" she said.

Nothing about this is "great"!

Seeing as I was being uncharacteristically feisty, I looked at the five sinister-looking men who stood before me and genuinely worried about the future. At this point, I didn't know if I would make it home alive. In fact, I feared that the house was a bandit's hideout for a second and glanced at Rose out of fear.

"Hm? What's up, Usato? Oh, right. Ya don't know their names. Fellas, introductions."

Yup, I'm pretty sure that this lady has no idea what I'm thinking. I genuinely doubt that she's scared of these men. Oh, wait—she's the team captain, so she's just like them in a way. Now the scary-looking men are surrounding me. What are they doing? W-Wait, I'll get down on all fours and apologize, just please let me live!

The tallest man of the bunch stepped forward. "The name's Tong. I specialize in sterilization. At your service, new kid," he said, his voice incredibly deep. He wore a twisted grin as sweat dripped down his face.

Sterilization? Yeah right! Only if it's with a flamethrower, I bet!

After that, the other men introduced themselves one by one.

"I'm Mill. At your service, new kid."

"I'm Alec. At your service, new kid."

"I'm Gomul. At your service, new kid."

"I'm Gurd. At your service, new kid."

I started crying. "I-I'm s-sorry . . ."

Crying isn't cool when you're a second-year in high school, but in my defense I think just about anyone would cry in a situation like this. I was surrounded by scary-looking guys who'd cut off all escape routes and were coming at me with introductions from every direction. What was I—a sacrifice? Was I a sacrifice to them?!

Anybody who wouldn't cry in this situation is nuts!

"Hey, knock it off! Quit scaring the new guy!" Rose shouted.

Tong let out a yelp of pain and was gone. Rose had kicked him across the room. Putting a hand to her head in frustration, she yelled at the other four men through clenched teeth.

Honestly, **you** *scare me the most!*

"As long as yer nice to him, I don't care. Do I make myself clear?

"We were only tryna welcome him, Sister Rose!" said the stout man named Mill. I was downright in a state of shock.

This is what they call a warm welcome?!

Their warped view of hospitality sent shivers down my spine and I couldn't hide it.

Rose punted Mill across the room too, then shifted her piercing gaze back to me.

"Oh, brother. Usato, these guys aren't healers but they're still my subordinates. Their main duty is to secure injured soldiers on the front lines. There are two others who can use healing magic, but unfortunately, they're working somewhere else at the moment. That's why I'm gonna teach you healing magic myself."

"Huh?"

"That's not a proper response."

"Y-Yes, ma'am!"

"Good. We'll start your training tomorrow. You can stay in . . . Tong's room. It's not being used, is it, Tong?"

Did my freedom just fly out the window?

"I'm the only one in my room."

"Okay, good. Give him the lowdown. It's late so get your asses to bed."

"Yes, ma'am!" they shouted.

"Yes, ma'am . . ." I said.

"Follow me. I'll show you to your room," said Tong.

So, I did exactly that. The room was surprisingly . . . normal. It was clean, organized, and relatively minimalistic. I sat down on a bed, marveling at how different it was from my room back on Earth. I was surprised, to say the least. I figured there would at least be some chains and flamethrowers lying around.

"Hey, new kid," Tong said suddenly.

I found myself shaking because I wasn't expecting him to speak. "Yes, sir?" I answered, still trembling. He was incredibly tall, which made him rather intimidating.

"Don't call me sir. No need to be formal 'round me."

"Okay."

Mustering the confidence to answer him was mentally draining.

Just then, Tong threw me some plain-looking clothes.

"Use these clothes when yer training. Ya got three outfits right there, so switch out the pants and shirts when you can. The bathroom's just down the hallway. Any other questions and you'll have to ask sister."

"Th-Thanks."

I'd been wearing my stuffy school uniform this whole time, so I was happy to have some regular clothes. I changed into my new clothes and put the old ones away where Tong had told me to put them.

Tong was already lying in bed, facing away from me.

What the hell. He's not a brute. He's just shy, isn't he? Damn tsundere.

"Training kills so you'll wanna sleep early. 'Specially yer healing training. Tomorrow's gonna be hell."

"H-Hell?"

"You can heal yer own wounds with that magic . . . if you catch my drift."

Oh. Does that mean I'll have to keep training even if I get injured?

I felt all the blood drain from my face. Because I could heal my own wounds, I doubted that Rose would let me rest. Even so, she was the head honcho. Before learning healing magic from her, I wanted to practice a little. I wasn't there on my own volition, but if she was going to teach me healing magic anyway, being her apprentice didn't sound like a bad idea.

"Can you teach me what 'healing magic' is all about?"

This was my chance. I was in another world where I could learn a technique that would give me extraordinary power. I didn't know what the future would bring, but at the very least I wanted to enjoy the fantastical life I'd always dreamed of. Plus, if I completed this training, I could support Kazuki and Inukami.

"What? Tch. For Pete's sake, listen up," Tong barked. "Here's the lowdown. If I'm being nice, I'd say healers are mages who are good at healing. But if I'm being blunt, I'd say they're mages who don't got no skills."

"No . . . skills?"

"Yeah. They're walking targets on the battlefield since offensive magic ain't their thing. They were treated like trash in this country until a few years ago, but even now other countries still treat 'em like they're useless."

It made sense. I could see how healers would be targeted on the battlefield and treated like trash. Even **I** killed healers first in all my games.

"Hell, I used to think healers were small fries . . . until everything changed," he went on.

"What changed?"

"I said too much. Goodnight."

"Hey, no fair! Don't leave me hanging!"

"Shut yer trap and go to sleep, dumbass!" yelled Tong. He slumped back into bed.

You don't have to yell at me like that, you know.

Feeling shaken, I cried a little in bed as I prepared myself for my first day of training.

CHAPTER 2

The Beginning of Hell!

Rose told me to keep a diary, so I'm writing my first entry today. I can't write in their language, but that's a good thing—this means that everything I put in this journal will stay my little secret. This looks like the perfect place to log my daily gripes.

Day One

To kick off this diary, I'll write about what happened today.

The "hellish training" Tong mentioned yesterday was surprisingly easy. First, I had to "feel" magic, which was pretty simple to do. It felt like something warm is welling up in my chest. Rose-san said that I'll learn how to release magic from my body next time.

After I finished magic practice, it was time for me to study up on this world. I was sat at a desk and handed massive books. There was only one instruction from Rose-san: read. That was an especially ridiculous request from my teacher.

When I told her there's no point in studying since I can't read their language, she just yelled at me and said that everyone brought here by the hero summoning is gifted with automatic translating magic. And as it turns out . . . I can read after all. Magic is truly amazing.

According to my books, monsters are said to inhabit this world. It's so on brand for a sent-to-another-world story that I practically squealed. But Rose-san punched me for that. It hurt like hell.

Another thing I learned while I was quietly reading is that there are a great number of races in this world—even races I've seen in video games! I also found out that there are many other countries besides Llinger Kingdom, but most of them are run by humans. How boring.

Rose-san silently watched me as I read those massive books. It's the worst kind of peer pressure. But I mean, if this is what her training is like every day, I'm pretty sure I can do this. Though it does worry me that Tong always looks like he feels bad for me.

Oh well, I'll just have to work hard again tomorrow.

Day Two
Ran like hell.

Day Three
Rose-san never lets me take breaks. All she does is heal me and make me run until I fall down from exhaustion.

This lady is seriously insane. She's always telling me to "train my legs" because it "won't kill me" and that I should feel magic while I'm running. I'm not really sure why. In any case, this isn't exactly what I'd thought magic training would be.

When I told her that I'm not her damn slave, all she said was "Train like yer dying. If you kick the bucket, I'll bring you back." That dang lady won't even let a guy rest when he's dead! After that, I prostrated on the ground before Rose-san and begged her to save me.

"My legs feel like lead and I can't go on any longer!" I cried. But all

she did was slap my thigh without saying a word. I was so busy rolling on the ground in pain that I almost didn't realize that my legs didn't hurt anymore after that.

She said, "I healed your pain by force. Now get running, you waste of a human."

How crazy is that?

Day Four

Today I trained with the other team members . . . but it was more like training on steroids. You'd think they were training troops, not a "rescue team" or whatever. All of them were shouting weird things like "Oorah!" while they ran as fast as they could. Naturally, I can't keep up the pace.

When Rose-san saw me lagging behind, she yelled, "Hey, look who's as slow as a snail!"

Please save me, Kazuki. I'm gonna die before I learn how to use healing magic.

Day Five

I almost think Kazuki received my telepathic SOS because today he and Inukami-senpai came to visit. Apparently, they've been training at the castle. One of their teachers is Welcie-san, the mage, and the other is Siglis-san, the army commander.

They said that Siglis-san is really strict but a good person at heart. It also seems that Celia, the king's daughter, has been attending Kazuki's lessons. I wonder what that's all about. They asked me what I've been doing, and I simply told them I've been running. Kazuki didn't seem convinced but Inukami-senpai gasped the moment she looked at my legs.

"Let me touch them," she said. But she was breathing really heavily, so I just ignored her. They're both working hard. I've gotta try to keep up.

Day Six

I ran again today.

When I was running, I noticed that a pale green light was emanating from my hand. There was only one question on my mind: "Do I really need this right now?" Rose-san was being a cold-hearted, ruthless hag as usual (lol).

She can't read what I'm writing, so I can talk all the smack I want.

Day Seven

Does that lady have ESP? Or maybe it was painted all over my face.
Well, for whatever reason, Rose held me captive and made me run until I thought I was dead. It was so bad that I thought I was losing my mind. She said she was miffed and plans to make my training harder.

What the hell? Curse that overpowered gorilla. One day I'll get my revenge.

Day Eight

Me too dumb to learn anything.

Day Nine

*I . . . need . . . healing. I . . . **really** . . . need healing.*

Day Ten

I can tell that I'm growing mentally stronger. Ever since I learned how to release healing magic from my body, I can run all I want and never feel tired. Rose is making me lean and mean, though. To say her methods are strange is an understatement.

It has been ten days since I started training under Rose-san. When I first started, I worked hard because I wanted to learn magic and support Kazuki and Inukami-senpai. At this point, I can't help but wonder something: Can an average guy like me really support them when their magic and talents are on a whole other level? I'm not so sure anymore.

I don't want Rose-san to punch me if I tell her how I'm feeling, but at the same time I feel like I'm losing sight of my goal. On a brighter note, I'm training for the rescue team and I am here of my own volition.

*Rose-san may have brought me here against my will, but there's no way I'll let myself run away now. I **will** complete her training. I'll show her what I'm made of.*

Now that I think about it, "Rose-san" is unwieldy.

I'll just call her "Rose" from now on.

Day Eleven

A new training regimen started today. I had to do push-ups—one thousand of them. I healed myself as I breezed through the training. For some reason, Rose seemed satisfied with my progress. Maybe she was just smiling because something was stuck to my face.

I completed the training and was barely yelled at today. I'm honestly scared at how happy that makes me. It's not normal to fist pump because I didn't get yelled at, but that's exactly what I did.

Day Twelve
I ran from morning to noon, then did push-ups until dusk. I don't have much else to say, except that recently my body feels as light as a feather.

Day Thirteen
Rose noticed my progress and attached weights to my body. They weigh a ton. The kingdom guards look horrified when they see me, but I just keep looking straight ahead.

Day Fourteen
That asshole Tong ate my lunch!
    He's gonna pay.
    I'll get back at him later.
    I also remembered that it's been two weeks since I first started training. I'm somehow getting through it. Running doesn't hurt anymore and I got used to the weights pretty quickly.

Wait. Am I being brainwashed or something?

*   *   *

More than three weeks had passed since Kazuki, Usato, and I

were summoned to this world. Because I'd absorbed myself in training, I felt like I could fight well enough. But, then again, I'd never been in a real fight. I didn't know if I could actually win.

On one particular morning, I had finished my training and had started eating lunch in a corner of the training area, under the shade of a tree with Kazuki.

"You've gotten a lot stronger, Kazuki-kun," I said.

"I'm still nowhere near as strong as you, senpai," he replied.

Kazuki wasn't the only one growing at an almost inhuman speed. I was now strong enough to spar with the Llinger Kingdom's strongest knight, Siglis, and the brilliant mage Welcie. On the one hand, I knew they were going easy on me. On the other hand, they were genuinely surprised by how fast I'd improved.

But deep down it simply wasn't enough.

To me, the magic in this country simply wasn't exciting enough. Throwing out some lightning bolts was enough to make the crowd go wild. Their cheers made Kazuki blush, but not me. I wanted to master long-range attacks that would send the battlefield reeling, to dish out lightning punches and other abnormal techniques.

"Guess I'll just have to make them myself," I said.

"Whatever do you mean?" a voice said in reply.

All I was thinking was: "Uh-oh. I didn't mean to say that out loud."

The girl who had spoken was none other than Celia Vulgast Llinger, the king's golden-haired daughter. Even though she was the royal princess, she had been with us ever since Rose took Usato away.

Back then, King Lloyd had decided that bringing him back would be too hard. He assigned two teachers to Kazuki and me: One of them was Siglis, the army commander, and the other was Welcie, the kingdom mage who was known for her powerful spells. Along with our teachers, the king had also summoned his daughter, Celia, and had introduced her to us. We were all about the same age, so we've stuck together ever since.

Kazuki heaved a sigh.

He had just finished lunch and was gazing at the scenery outside the castle.

Hmm, judging by that listless stare, I bet he's worrying about Usato.

"I wonder what Usato's up to?" he asked.

Yup. So easy to read.

The last time we saw Usato he was being worked to the bone. At the time, I couldn't tell if he was having trouble adjusting to life in this world or if rescue-team training was as demanding as it seemed.

"If you don't mind me asking, what kind of person is Usato-sama?" asked Celia, seemingly curious about him.

Before I got to answer, Kazuki puffed out his chest and started talking.

"Hm? Oh! He's a friend who came with us to this world,

but we only became friends right before we were summoned."

"Seeing how happy you are really does make me think that you have no other guys to hang out with."

"Th-That's not true!"

Kazuki insecurely muttered that he does, in fact, have friends, which made Celia giggle. But I knew the truth. The guys at school always kept their distance from Kazuki. Even if they'd only just become friends, Usato was an important friend to Kazuki, nonetheless.

"Where is he now?" Celia asked.

"The rescue team, I think? Yeah. He's with them," Kazuki replied.

"D-Did you just say the rescue team?!" she exclaimed.

"That's where he is, right, senpai?" Kazuki said.

"Yeah," I confirmed.

I had noticed something curious the last time I saw Usato. As someone who had mastered all sorts of sports back on Earth, I knew a lot about the human body, and I knew even more about muscles. But Usato's arms were so built that they were unrecognizable. Even though he'd only trained for one week, his chest was already as buff as his arms.

If he'd have just let me feel his muscles, I would've known how built he was, but Usato refused 'cause he's a big meanie. In any case, training so aggressively—and so suddenly—isn't good for the body.

"I'm worried about him." I murmured.

"Senpai?" Kazuki looked concerned.

"No, it's nothing," I said, quickly brushing him off. "Anyway, you were surprised when we mentioned the rescue team, Celia. Did something happen over there?"

"Well, you see, strange rumors about the rescue team have been spreading through the castle lately."

"What kind of rumors?"

She must know what they are. Why else would she refuse to look us in the eyes after hearing he's with the rescue team? Did something terrible happen to him?

"This is just hearsay," Celia whispered, "but I hear that their training is so rigorous that all the members scream in agony, yet the new trainee powers through it without making a peep. I overheard the soldiers talking about it earlier."

"Okay, now I'm really worried. Can we wrap up our training for today and go check on Usato-kun?" I said, my face hardening with concern.

"Yeah. I'll go too." Kazuki wore the same grimace and nodded.

Kazuki and I skipped our afternoon training and headed to the rescue team quarters with Celia. Having the princess leave the castle without a guard would be dangerous, so Siglis escorted us there.

The rescue team quarters stood amid lush, vibrant trees.

There were no people in sight. It was a little eerie, since Usato wasn't standing in front of the building like he had been when we'd visited the other day.

"Is Usato-sama here?" Celia asked.

"He's supposed to be, but I don't see him," I said.

"Think he's in the middle of afternoon training?" Kazuki wondered.

"Well, why don't we find him? If we interrupt their training, we can simply go back to the castle. Siglis-san, won't you lead the way?" I asked Siglis.

"As you wish. Follow me," he answered.

Eager to quickly check on Usato, we followed Siglis through the lush trees to the rescue team training grounds. Celia's eyes sparkled as she took in the outdoors. She was normally secluded in the castle and must have been excited by this change of scenery.

"Wow! This is incredible, Kazuki-sama!" she exclaimed.

"Celia-sama, you must stay close to me at all times," Siglis reminded her.

"Oh Siglis, don't be so overprotective!" she quipped.

She was the country's princess, after all. I could understand why he was being overprotective. Siglis continued leading the way wearing a troubled expression.

"Sorry about all this, Siglis-san."

"No need to apologize. I have matters to discuss with Rose,

so it is no trouble at all. The training grounds are up ahead. I believe that is where Usato-sama will be," Siglis said, pointing straight ahead.

"Okay!" Kazuki replied.

I had just been wondering how much Usato had improved since I last saw him when we stepped out of the woods. Siglis was pointing. I looked in that direction and saw a clearing about thirty meters wide. Usato was doing push-ups right in the middle of it. Kazuki and I should've shouted for joy as we stood side by side, but we didn't. We were totally silent.

"What is the matter?" Celia asked. "What in the world is going on?!"

Huff! Huff! Huff! Huff! Huff!

Usato was doing push-ups . . . with a giant boulder on his back! It looked like it was about fifty kilograms. Usato was literally shouldering that boulder by himself. Sitting proudly on top of it was the rescue team captain, Rose!

"Yo. You're slowin' down, ya damn slug. Gonna give up just 'cause I gave you more weight?" Rose slyly remarked.

"Who the hell said . . . that I'm giving up?!" Usato hissed.

"Save your breath." Rose said bluntly.

"Tch." Usato was too annoyed to respond.

Did he just talk back to Rose? Is that really you in there, Usato? Is this the same boy we had fun banter with right before we were summoned? Where did that sweet Usato go?

"Oh? Did I just hear you say 'tch,' like yer angry or somethin'?" Rose mused.

"You're so light I forgot you were there, Rose-san. It slipped out by accident."

"Aww, I'm light. What a nice thing to say. If it's that easy for you, why don't we add summore weight?" Rose stepped onto the ground. Then she picked up an enormous cement block nearby and effortlessly chucked it onto Usato's back.

The block fell on him with a *thud*, his arms shaking as his body sunk to the ground. Even so, he wouldn't be bested; he gnashed his teeth together and continued doing push-ups. As Rose watched him do this, she broke into a satisfied grin.

"You know what? Yer really becoming my type of man. At this rate, I'll be able to take ya there in no time. Hm? What're you doing here?" Rose said, finally noticing us.

Did she just say he's her type? Don't tell me she's forcing this grueling training on him to make him her ideal man.

We were all at a total loss. Instead of walking into a fantastical adventure, we had walked into an intense scene about training in martial arts. Kazuki rubbed his eyes in disbelief, wondering if what he'd seen was a dream. I was also dumbfounded myself.

Usato looked like an average high schooler, yet here he was doing push-ups. His eyes gleamed with anger. After seeing this, who wouldn't want to run in fear? As this scene unfolded before us, army commander Siglis angrily walked toward Rose.

"Hey. What's an old fart like you doing here, Siglis? Why'd you bring the heroes and the princess to my turf?" Rose asked casually.

"What the hell do you think you're doing?" Siglis fumed.

"Hm?" Rose seemed confused.

"I said, what the **hell** do you think you're doing?!" Siglis shouted as he grabbed her by the collar. "Breaking the spirits of promising young men? You should be ashamed!"

I could understand why Siglis was angry. What she was subjecting Usato to wasn't "training." It was torture. As Siglis firmly grasped Rose's collar, she reverted to a blank expression and then grabbed him by the arm. His armor crinkled loudly and twisted in her hand, but he held her collar tight without so much as glancing at the warping armor.

"Get your hands off me," she said bluntly. "You gotta grand sense of chivalry, I get it. But don't you dare try forcing that shit on me. I do things my own way, and this here's my right-hand man. Wouldn't be the case if he couldn't clear these easy trials."

"Right-hand . . . man?" Siglis looked confused.

"That's right. This kid's a diamond in the rough. He perseveres like a champ and never calls it quits. He's got what it takes to clear my training. Already has my stamp of approval."

My eyes met Rose's and I backed away without thinking. She was looking in my direction, but she wasn't really looking at me. She was focused on something else. All I knew was that her eyes were filled with contradiction.

"You swine! The king ordered us to reenlist you in the army, but I simply will not tolerate this behavior!" Siglis shouted.

"Hah! Can't open my right eye, so couldn't do it anyway." Rose pointed to her right eye, which was permanently sealed shut.

Is she using the damage to her eye as an excuse to stay out of the army? From what I hear from King Lloyd and Welcie, they wouldn't care about the injury since she has talent.

"Enough of this nonsense!" Siglis huffed. He walked toward us, looking worried. "Princess Celia, I must take my leave. Stay close to Kazuki-sama at all costs."

"Huh? Huhhh?" the princess said in disbelief.

"I will return as soon as I have calmed down," Siglis said.

After he uttered those parting words, Siglis disappeared into the woods. He seemed to have left to avoid fighting with Rose.

"Welp, there goes Siglis. Do the heroes or princess got any problems with my training?"

"They don't care about that!" Usato shouted. "Yo, Rose. What happened just now?! Did you call me your 'right-hand man'? Oh joy. I'm soooo happy. Here, let me give you a right-hand knuckle sandwich to show my appreciation. C'mon, what's the hold up? If you want a right-hand man, then hurry up and stick out your face!"

"Not before I give you my own present first . . . but that'll have to come later. These heroes came all this way so they must wanna talk. Take a break with them and eat lunch," Rose said, shoving her right fist in Usato's face.

The moment she looked at us she put down her fist. Her whole demeanor had changed. We watched her walk toward the quarters, then we approached Usato. He removed the weight on his back, put it on the ground, and stretched out.

"Are you okay?" I asked.

"Yeah, but who's this?" Usato said, looking at Celia.

"My name is Celia Vulgast Llinger. Please call me Celia, Usato-sama."

"Usato . . . sama? Aren't you the king's . . ."

"Yes, I am his daughter."

Usato became a bit flustered. He probably wasn't used to women adding a "-sama" to his name, which is exactly how Kazuki had felt the first few times it had happened to him. Celia asked Usato to treat her like an ordinary person, and he reluctantly acquiesced.

"So, what's your training like, Kazuki? I can tell you've both gotten stronger," Usato said.

No one said a word.

"Why so silent?" he asked.

I couldn't tell him. I couldn't tell him that our training was nowhere near as brutal as his. It wasn't a walk in the park, but it was nothing compared to his.

Our training was designed to avoid putting unnecessary strain on our bodies—a carefully weaved, efficient plan that would improve our fighting expertise. In other words, it was the total opposite of Usato's experience. His training was dangerous, made him do the impossible, and actively pushed him past his limits.

After hearing all the rumors and seeing Usato's insane training regimen in person, one could safely assume that he had been training like this for the past three weeks. His profile didn't look all that different, but I could tell that his body had gotten incredibly strong over the past three weeks.

Let's take a peek.

I lifted up Usato's shirt without thinking.

"You don't mind, right, Usato-kun?"

"What? What are you doing Inukami senpaaahh?!"

I rolled up the shirt he was wearing as Celia's cheeks turned bright red.

I see. He bruises his muscles through excessive training and then heals them with magic. That must be why he's so built. On top of his incredible stamina, he also wields incredible strength. It's almost like he's superhuman.

"I really underestimated you, Usato-kun! Your muscles are stellar!" I exclaimed.

"Aren't you a little **too** excited, Inukami-senpai?" Usato asked.

"Oh no, I mean, I'm just impressed that you've become this strong in such a short period of time."

He had survived training that was grueling at best.

"Kazuki-sama, is Suzune-sama okay?" Celia asked innocently.

"Sorry, Celia," Kazuki said, "but I have no idea."

Usato peeled me off of him with both arms, seemingly irritated that I wouldn't let go. As much as it pained me to leave his muscles, it was probably better that I stayed away.

"Whew. Anyway, I'm glad you two seem to be doing all right," Usato said.

"You seem . . . like you're doing well too, Usato," Kazuki responded.

"Ha ha ha! That seems to be my only redeeming feature nowadays," Usato answered. He cheerfully smiled and didn't look tired at all.

"I guess we had no reason to worry after all." Kazuki breathed a sigh of relief.

"Worry about what?" Usato asked. "Eh, never mind. Next time I wanna go visit you guys. I'd love to see what training's like at the castle." He looked far off toward the castle.

"He mustn't," Celia shuddered.

Celia didn't want Usato to see the knights train since he was under the assumption that they trained as hard as he did. Seeing him would undoubtedly lower their morale.

"Is your training always like this, Usato?" asked Kazuki.

"Yeah." Usato shyly scratched his head. "But today was a lot easier than usual."

"**That** was the easy part?"

That's terrifying. I wonder how this is affecting his mental health. I mean, he's an average high schooler who had nothing to do with this world, but they dragged him here and now the rescue team is forcing him to complete cruel, demanding training. I'm sure he has his complaints.

"Aren't you tired, Usato?" asked Kazuki.

I had been thinking the very same thing.

"Huh?" Usato seemed perplexed. After contemplating the question for a few brief seconds, Usato answered immediately. "I'm incredibly tired. When I first got here, all I wanted to do was escape."

Kazuki followed up with a question. "Do you still feel that way now?"

Usato nodded, then opened up his right hand. We watched as beautiful green magic emerged from his palm.

"The captain's scary as hell but I no longer feel like I want to escape. Healing magic might've put me through the ringer, but it's the reason that this tiring training has become kinda fun. Plus, living here isn't too much of a drag. The guys are too loud sometimes, but I deal with it," said Usato, grinning wryly. His resilience was impressive.

"You're amazing. Looks like you've finally found where you belong," I said.

"I'm really not. I only powered through my training because I didn't want to bother you on the battlefield, senpai," Usato answered.

"You'd never bother us," Kazuki protested.

It was hard to believe that he had actually disagreed with Usato. I'd never thought of Usato as a "bother," but I could see how being accidentally dragged to this world could make him feel like a hindrance.

Or, at least, that's how I thought he had felt. Instead, he only grinned in response.

"Nah, I'm just sticking it out because I'm stubborn. In the end, you're the heroes who have to fight the Demon Lord's army. No way am I gonna be the only one slacking off."

"But you don't have to fight the Demon Lord's army, Usato," Kazuki said.

"And I'm not ready to fight them. But even so, I can't just stand here and do nothing. If I don't work hard at **something**, it wouldn't be fair to you both."

Stubborn, huh? I see. Guess there's nothing we can do about that. This is his decision and it isn't our place—or anyone else's—to try to change his mind.

"In that case, Usato-kun, if I'm ever in trouble, come save me, okay?" I teased.

"Um . . . How do you expect me to react when you suddenly act like a normal girl?"

"I **am** a normal girl! What else would I be?!"

"I certainly think it would be hard to classify you as a normal girl, Suzune-sama," Celia added.

Not even Celia's on my side.

Everyone—even Kazuki—laughed and the conversation came to a close.

Wait. That was fun? Why did I have to be the butt of the joke?!

A little while later, we were in the middle of a conversation when a full-grown man emerged from the woods. He was carrying a lunch box in one hand.

"Yo, Usato! Look at how nice I am, bringin' you lunch!" the man said.

At that moment, a vein pulsated furiously in Usato's forehead. I thought Usato was mild-mannered, so seeing him turn into a raging demon almost felt like a bad dream.

However, this wasn't a dream, and reality wasn't so kind.

"You got some nerve saying shit like that, blockhead!" Usato shouted. "Don't have enough brains to remember the shit you pulled last week, do ya?!"

"Ugh! I dunno whut yer sayin'! Try speakin' words a simple guy like me would know, dumbass!"

"If I make this any easier it'll be like talkin' to a baby! Oh, right! Must be because you got hot air for brains!"

"Damn punk! Can never let go of things, can ya?!"

"That's rich coming from the guy who ate this 'damn punk's' lunch!"

Usato suddenly closed the distance between them and kicked the tall, rugged man. The man safely parried the kick, the corners of his mouth trembling as he glared at Usato.

"The hell! What would you do if that hit me? I'm stronger than you by a longshot. I'll mess you up before big sis even sees you!"

"Hah! Think you can? Bring it on!"

Usato and the stern-looking man started to scuffle. Kazuki was standing next to me. He looked troubled at first, but then started laughing out loud.

"So, **this** is what Usato's daily life is like!"

"Yeah. He's doing his best in this place," I added.

*Looks like I was worried for nothing. He's surviving almost **too** well in this world, even better than us! But I think this place might be making him a little crazy.*

"Listen, I can't just stand here after that. Let's go back to the castle and train!" Kazuki exclaimed. Watching Usato train must have made him feel antsy to jump back into action.

"Oh my! Please slow down, Sir Kazuki!" cried Celia, chasing after him.

I watched them run away, then looked back at Usato once more.

He might say that being dragged into the hero-summoning and becoming a healer was just a coincidence, but I think this happened for a reason.

As I watched the two men fight, I whispered softly. "Let's give it our all, Usato-kun."

CHAPTER 3

Beyond Cruel! It's the Darkness of Llinger!

More than one month had passed since Rose made me join the rescue team. In that short span of time, my body had drastically changed.

First, I became incredibly strong. That much I knew. My hellish, intensive training had finally borne fruit. Over time I mastered running, push-ups, and weight lifting. In other words, I was now a lean, mean fighting machine. My body would have never changed so radically if I were back home.

According to Rose, the reason our training was so intensive was to make sure we could escape quickly from the battlefield. Her motto was basically: The faster we run, the sooner we can save lives. The mission of the rescue team—and the healers who belonged to it—was to save those who were hurt or closest to death. We were told to heal anyone we could. But doing so was incredibly tough. We literally had to carry wounded men, who had been abandoned on the battlefield, to safety. Without courage and strength, it wasn't even worth trying.

I couldn't help but think, "Can a guy like me really do something that crazy?"

But I didn't want to bear the burden of being a hero— of being tasked to save the country like Inukami or Kazuki. I wanted to help them, but I still didn't know how I would do it.

I wasn't ready for what lay ahead. No matter how strong I became, I just couldn't imagine being thrown onto the battlefield.

Every morning, I would wake up and sigh. I would always feel so insecure before training. But then I would move my body and see the training was clearly working. Even so, I still doubted that I had the mental fortitude to match the strength I had gained.

Realizing how pathetic I sounded, I slapped myself in the face.

"Worrying won't solve anything. I just have to keep trying," I said.

Today I had training, just like I did the day before. I could see that it was working and I was full of motivation.

All right. I'll think about mental fortitude and all that stuff later. Nothing's gonna change if I sit here worrying after all.

I got out of bed, changed my clothes, then opened the door to my room.

So, what kinda training will we have today?

"We're going out," Rose stated.

What? No training? Then give me back my motivation!

The sad truth was that the only places I knew about in this new world were confined to the inside of the rescue team's training grounds (since I'd been kidnapped the day I was summoned and all). I didn't know what Rose was planning, but I followed her anyway. The other members had mandatory training, so they didn't come with us.

Sucks for them. Bahaha.

"Carry this," Rose commanded.

She handed me a backpack that was practically as tall as me. Without a word, she left and started heading to town.

Hm? What's wrong, Tong? Why do you look as if you're watching a soldier march to his death? If there's nothing to worry about, then whatever.

"What's the hold up? Get over here," she said impatiently.

Rose was waiting for me by the entrance to the castle town. I had a bad feeling about this. A **really** bad feeling. But resisting her would just cause trouble, so I quietly followed her lead. Still carrying the big backpack, I ran after Rose.

When I finally caught up, I started walking a few paces behind her, taking in the view that had shifted from a lush, vivid forest to a bustling town. It was my first time in the castle town and it was invigorating to say the least. The town didn't have the same devices or scientific advancements we had back on Earth. If anything, it reminded me of a quaint marketplace I once visited when I was a kid.

"Llinger Kingdom is a flourishing center of trade. Many come here from other countries to work," Rose said.

"I see. Huh?" I noticed something unusual.

A fox-eared girl was tending a shop that sold pointy fruits, but something about the way she moved seemed suspicious. I figured that she must be a beastkin. In any case, seeing one for the very first time left me speechless.

"Quit staring at the beastkin, you idiot. I know you've never seen one before, but it just makes 'em uncomfortable," Rose nagged.

"Oh, sorry." I quickly apologized.

She's not a freak show or something, so I should stop looking unless I wanna be rude.

I attempted to look away from the girl, but our eyes suddenly met. She was staring right at me with a blank expression on her face.

I don't know what she's thinking, but. . .

"Cute girls make everything better" I said.

"What're you sayin'? You a pervert or somethin'?" Rose quipped.

No way! I can do without the insults, you know. Actually, why is she the only beastkin girl around here?

"If people come here from other countries to work, I don't see why there shouldn't be more demihumans or beastkin around," I noted.

"This country lets in demihumans pretty easily. Mainly 'cause His Majesty's got a kind heart. It's the road here that's trouble. Scum like thieves, kidnappers, and assassins target 'em. Some demihumans, especially beastkin, possess valuable powers. Since they look so demure, they're often sold as slaves for a hefty profit," she explained.

"Slaves?" I stammered.

"This country doesn't have a system of institutionalized slavery, but there are places that use slaves. Know what I mean?" she continued.

"Yeah, I guess," I answered solemnly.

I understood what she meant, but it just didn't feel right. It was too disturbing for an ordinary guy like me to accept.

I looked at a world map the other day. From what I remember, the beastkin country is far away from Llinger Kingdom.

"Did they risk their lives to come here?" I asked.

"Yeah. Anyway, on to the next place," Rose said curtly.

I had no idea where she was going, but that was nothing new.

When I looked back at the fox girl, she was staring right at me. She just kept staring, and staring . . .

That's kinda creepy. Time to pick up the pace.

I followed Rose through the town without looking back. I was so absorbed in my surroundings, and busy wondering where we were going, that I hardly noticed when we ended up arriving at a large door on the outskirts of town.

Huh. Must be another town through that door. They must make their towns right next to each other. No, wait. This isn't the exit to the town . . . it's the exit to the kingdom itself!

A guard was standing in front of the door.

In the past month, I'd noticed that Rose stared people

down as she spoke. She was already staring down the guard and he seemed pretty shaken.

"Yo," Rose said. "Been a while, Thomas."

"R-Rose-san! H-How can I h-help you today?!" the man stammered.

"Gonna show my trainee the outdoors," Rose answered.

What she really meant by that was "open the damn door." That was Rose for you. Her presence alone made gatekeepers shake in their boots.

"I-I'll open it now!" he exclaimed.

"Thanks," she said.

I decided to butt in.

"Spoken like a true mobster, Rose-san. Er, ya know what? Never mind."

We'd been together for a whole month, so I knew how to avoid setting her off. The light faded from the guard's eyes as he opened the door. I felt bad for the gloomy gatekeeper as I bowed to him and walked toward the door.

Rose and I passed through the doorway together.

"Where are we going, Rose-san?" I asked.

"To a forest filled with monsters," she said casually.

"What?" I was taken aback.

"Should be a few hours from here," she noted.

Excuse me! What are you talking about? Wait . . . is this backpack a freaking tent?! Are you making me stay in a forest packed with prowling monsters? What a damn ruthless ogre!

My eyes flitted back and forth nervously, but Rose just ignored me and quickly picked up the pace.

Wait. She didn't say I had to stay here, so maybe it's all in my head. C'mon, me. We can't give up hope yet.

* * *

I stood on a cliff, gazing into the murky forest that expanded below me. I glanced back at Rose, who was folding her arms, before my gaze returned to the forest.

"Some call it 'The Darkness of Llinger.' Others call it the 'Den of the Beasts.' You ain't leavin' until you hunt a Grand Grizzly. I don't care how long it takes," Rose instructed.

So not only do I have to survive, but I also have homework?!

"Grand Grizzly? Isn't that the monster a Blue Grizzly turns into after one hundred years?! **That** dangerous thing?! But they're deadly even before they grow up! It said so in my books! What the hell?! Do you hate me or something?!" I shouted.

"'Course I don't," she said calmly.

"Liar!" I yelled.

"Ugh, put a sock in it already. By now you should be able to kill a Grand Grizzly no problem. You get me?" she asked.

"No, I don't get you, I . . . Waiiiit, stop! Put me down!"

I shook my head violently, but Rose didn't care. She lifted me and the giant backpack off the ground like it was nothing.

Just how strong is this she-hulk?! Gah! Quit lifting me over your head like you're a baseball player or something!

"Unh!" she grunted.

"Gaaaaaaaah!" And with that, I went flying.

Her throw was so overpowered that I found myself spinning high into the air.

Is this how I die? Cause of death: thrown by the rescue team captain. Screw that! You've gotta be kidding me.

I suddenly ran out of momentum and began my descent. Below me was an overgrown forest of trees.

Die? Like hell I will!

I looked up at the sky and regained my balance. I'd found the key: my big backpack! Realizing that it would soften my fall, I shielded my face with my arms and steeled myself for impact.

"Gahhh?!"

I fell into the trees, but the impact of the fall was a bit softer than expected. Luckily, the trees lessened the blow by a lot, so the impact was less forceful than it normally would have been. During the fall, I was whacked by more branches than I could count.

I had closed my eyes, but when I opened them, I suddenly saw the ground before me.

How did I end up facing down? Ack! If I fall like this, I'm a goner!

"I'm not gonna get hurt! Not after all that!"

I enveloped myself in healing magic and landed on the

ground on my hands and feet. I went a bit numb, but otherwise I was fine . . . until my vision blurred and I collapsed on my back. Using the backpack as a crutch, I managed to get back on my feet. I wasn't tired physically, but I **was** mentally drained.

"I'm alive? Thank goodness."

I could've been seriously hurt if it weren't for that backpack. If Rose hadn't brought it, I would've been done for. Even so, I wasn't grateful to her. If I didn't hunt down a Grand Grizzly, I knew she'd just toss me back to the forest again.

"I don't wanna admit it, but it's just as Rose said: Taking down a Grand Grizzly is the only thing I can do."

That bear's a measly two meters tall. I've already clawed my way out of hell, so a dumb little bear should be—

"GRAAAAAAAAH!" something snarled.

"Huh?!" I flinched in response.

A loud, ferocious roar rang out from somewhere deep in the forest. I heard footsteps approaching, so I ran out of there as fast as I could. After all, I wouldn't be **Usa**to if I couldn't run like an **usa**gi (rabbit)!

"Looks like people can't overpower monsters with strength! I'll have to work my gray brain cells to the fullest and come up with a killer tactic!" I said to myself.

"GRAAAAAAAAH!"

"It's right behind me!" I shrieked.

When I looked back, I saw drool dripping down a white

Grand Grizzly's face. It was about three meters behind me. I'd already stumbled upon my target, but it was a lot scarier than I'd imagined.

I've never seen a bear that has such huge claws and fangs—not even at a zoo!

"What do I do, what do I do, what do I do?!"

Things you can do when you encounter a bear:
1. Play dead. (The urban legend factor makes it sound true, but I feel like that'd just get me eaten.)
2. Ring a bell to scare it off. (No bell, so that's out.)
3. Run away. (I think my legs can do it.)

I had chosen my strategy. My only option was to run!

"No bear can match my speed!" I said gallantly.

"GRAAAAAAAAH!" it roared.

"It's coming! Ah, crap!" I lost heart.

I didn't have to turn around to know it was there. It was hot on my trail.

This information would've been helpful much earlier, but I just remembered a documentary that said bears can run up to forty to sixty kilometers per second. I wouldn't be surprised if it's the same with Grand Grizzlies. No, they can probably run faster than that, which likely means . . . I'm dead meat.

Wait. Snap out of it! My training's been hellish since I came to this world! Am I so weak that I'd let a bear chase me around just because the color of his fur's a bit different?

No! No freaking way!

Rose's hazing is **way** *scarier than this!*

"This bear is *bearly* a threat! Let's fight one-on-one! You wanna eat me? Come get me! You'll never catch me! Just try!" I taunted.

Then three different, distinctive snarls rang out.

"You brought your friends?! No fair!" I shouted.

Sneaky, sneaky.

When I looked behind me, I saw two more bears with blue fur running beside their friend, the Grand Grizzly.

How are there more?! They're a different size and color than the first one. These Blue Grizzlies are a pain in the ass! They're multiplying out of nowhere like matryoshkas or something!

"Shit! This backpack's slowing me down!" I said, panicking.

But I wasn't about to take it off, especially since it was probably filled with tools that would help me survive in the forest. It was incredibly heavy—I'd say it was almost 100 kilograms. I couldn't imagine what she'd put in the backpack, but this was Rose after all. It must have been helpful.

However . . .

"How long do I have to keep running?" I said to myself.

"GRAAAAAAAAH!" the bears bellowed.

All I wanted was to make it out of this forest alive.

*   *   *

It was night. Earlier that day, I was literally thrown into a peril-ous forest that was teeming with monsters. Now I was resting up in a tree, a full twenty meters from the ground. The branch I was sitting on was so thick and sturdy that it supported my weight, as well as the weight of the backpack.

My clothes were hanging on a thin branch to dry, so I was only wearing underwear. People would have probably called me a pervert . . . but there was a method to my madness. Grand and Blue Grizzlies had chased me around for three hours after Rose tossed me into the forest. I found it odd that I couldn't throw them off my trail no matter what I did, so I realized that they might be tracking my scent.

If it was my scent they were following, I thought it best to wash it off. After one hour of searching, I finally found something that looked like a waterfall and jumped in. Though I managed to shake the bears off my trail, I was also sopping wet. I wanted to dry my clothes somewhere safe, so I climbed a tall tree and that's how I ended up here.

"So dark . . ."

It was several hours past sunset. Judging by how hungry I was, I figured it was about eight or nine in the evening. The sky was pitch-black—I couldn't see a thing. I had no choice but to rely on the light of the moon, which was several times bigger than the one back on Earth. I heard a savage cry, possibly from a nocturnal monster prowling at night.

"Tch. Can't even light a fire."

Monsters would notice a fire. It might scare them off, but I didn't want to take the risk. Especially considering that the only things in the backpack were dried food, a pen and paper, a leather canteen, and a knife with a blade that was only twenty centimeters long. There were no tools that would help me start a fire, and food took up most of the space! I was glad I didn't have to starve, but this felt a little overboard.

"Yup, not good. Not good," I mumbled without thinking.

What's my next move?

My ultimate goal was to take down a Grand Grizzly. The issue was that no matter how confident I was in my strength, I still didn't know how to harness that power. Training in martial arts meant diddly-squat against monsters.

What do I do?

"I can either use . . ."

. . . A knife, a pad, or a pen. I also had wet clothes. I put on my semidry pants for the time being and hung the knife on my waist.

"If you want to win, you must first know your enemy."

First, I needed to come up with a plan and make the tree my home base. Luckily, there was a river nearby. I worried that it might be infested with parasites, but at that point all I could do was pray that they weren't there. I wanted to boil water, but I had to wait until morning since starting a fire was out of the question.

"This doesn't look good, but I'll prove I can make it."

I enveloped my tired body in weak healing magic. Before I fell asleep, I laid down on the thick branch and carved a message into it with the knife.

"Day one complete."

I was alone, and I was going to have to fight by myself.

The next morning, I softened the dried food with water and put on the clothes I wore for training. I equipped myself with the canteen and the knife, then stayed low as I ran through the forest.

The pad and pen were in my pocket. I was ready to take them out at any time.

"Where am I?"

I carved markings into the trees and continued searching the area.

I just took a bath in the river, so I shouldn't have to worry about my scent . . . if I'm lucky.

As far as I knew, there were many other monsters in that forest besides bears. I carefully searched the area that surrounded my base.

"Whoa! That's . . ."

There were four deep ruts in a tree. It looked a big something or other had carved it up with their claws. An animal that size was likely the Grand Grizzly from the previous day.

Caution was required when searching the area. I was about to take a step forward when I heard something rustling in the tall grass in front of me.

"Huh?!"

Is it a monster?

I slowly brandished my knife and approached the tall grass as I frantically wiped away the sweat on my forehead. I was prepared to escape. If it was a dangerous creature, running away was the plan. With a hard gulp, I used my other hand to part the tall grass.

"Kyu," something squeaked.

"Huh?" I was confused.

There was a black ball of fur on the ground.

Wait. It's not a ball of fur, it's a small animal!

It was something I'd never seen in Rose's books—a monster who had distinctive black fur and small ears that stood up like antennae.

"It's . . . a bunny rabbit."

It looked like a rabbit, but its beautiful black fur and mysterious, gleaming red eyes made it look more like a very realistic stuffed animal.

The black rabbit gazed at me with its round, red eyes as

it lay on the ground. It looked as if it was about to whimper again. Slightly perplexed, I cut through the tall grass and approached the rabbit. When I took a closer look, I noticed that its hind leg was covered in light red blood.

"Are you hurt?" I asked.

"Kyu." The rabbit nodded.

Does it understand human speech? Ya know what, I'm not gonna go there. Anything is possible in fantasy worlds after all.

I walked up to the rabbit and found its injury. There seemed to be a cut on his hind leg. It was probably attacked by another monster.

"Hold still."

A gentle green light emitted from my hand. I applied it to the wound. After a few seconds, I removed my hand and the injury was gone without a trace. I couldn't have done that if I hadn't trained. It was basically the first time I had healed something else.

"All better. Be careful out there."

After I patted the black rabbit's head, I stood up and started walking away. It was so cute that I almost wanted to take it back to my base, but I couldn't forget the mission: I had to hunt a Grand Grizzly. No time to be preoccupied with adorable rabbits. I told myself that leaving would be the best for us both.

However, the rabbit followed me. I silently took a step forward and the rabbit followed suit.

What's going on?

"Now listen up. If you stick with me, you're gonna be attacked by a Grand Grizzly! Do you happen to know where it is?" I asked.

"Kyu," it responded.

Motioning me to follow it with its head, the rabbit ran off. Feeling like a character from *Alice in Wonderland*, I chased after it just to see what would happen.

"Kyuuuu!"

It hopped deeper into the forest without so much as making a sound. I noticed that its ears were as straight as a needle as they pointed ahead.

Do its ears have radars or something? That's super adorable.

After following it for ten minutes, the rabbit suddenly stopped moving.

"What's wrong?"

"Kyu kyu." The rabbit climbed up my leg to my shoulder.

"Whoa! What're you doing?"

Its black fur ticked the nape of my neck. The rabbit itself was surprisingly light.

This little guy is just too adorable.

The black rabbit stood on my shoulder. Its ears bent forward as if it were pointing at something.

"Kyu."

"You want me to see what's ahead?" I asked.

This rabbit can really understand what I say! Oh well. It's a cutie, so I'm not gonna question it.

I parted some bushes before me with a *rustle* to reveal a dark cave and two Blue Grizz . . . lies?!

"What the—"

I covered my mouth.

Screaming now would alert the bears. But wow, they must live in that cave!

"Thanks. I really owe you one," I whispered to the rabbit on my shoulder.

Looking abashed at what I said, it started grooming itself. It was insanely adorable.

Now that I knew where the cave was, I took out my pad and my pen.

"Kyu?"

"Hm? Want to know what this is?"

Taking down a bear wasn't going to be easy.

If I was going to do it, I had to catch it off guard, which could only mean . . .

"A journal."

*All right. I'll start a journal that **will** save my life.*

Day Two

The black rabbit led me to the target's den. When we got there, I spotted two Blue Grizzlies and one Grand Grizzly.

One of the Blue Grizzlies is rather small. Judging by its mannerisms, I'd say it's a child. The other one is big. Probably the little one's parent.

My books said that Grand Grizzlies tend to live in groups. Is this a group too?

I stopped observing them after one hour since there were no new developments.

The rabbit stayed perched on my shoulder as usual. It's cute, so it can stay.

Day Three

I observed the den like I did yesterday.

No movement again.

Nothing unusual happened, so I ended up leaving.

Why does this rabbit keep following me? It understands what I say and possesses the unique ability to sense danger. It's incredibly handy.

I have so many questions.

But I'll just let it be 'cause it's cute.

Day Four

My stomach hurts.

Day Five

I knew it. The water's no good. Having the rabbit next to me as I suffered from stomach pains was extremely reassuring. I started feeling better in the afternoon, so I decided to go observe the bears then.

I camped out in a tree and saw that they were out hunting. I haven't seen them for a single day, but it feels like it's been ages since I last saw them. The Grand Grizzly likes to take the Blue Grizzly cub out hunting. It's actually kind of endearing.

Today I learned that they will basically eat anything. They easily bring down Fall Boars, which are wild boar monsters that have highly developed hind legs.

Will I really be able to take down the bear?

Day Six

I was attacked by a monster.

The black rabbit showed me where to find clean water, but on the way back to home base the rabbit started to tremble.

That's when an enormous snake that looked like a tsuchinoko appeared out of the blue. Its body is so thick and large that I'd guess it's a whopping seven meters long. Even so, it doesn't act like a snake. It headed straight for me. I truly felt scared from the pit of my soul. Naturally, I fled the scene as fast as I could.

It was insanely persistent in its pursuit, but I somehow managed to flee.

I even took a longer route back to base to play it safe.

There's something off about that snake. It's a lot more ominous than the other monsters I've seen. Heck, it even scared the black rabbit, and the little guy's never fazed when it sees a Grand Grizzly.

I don't know for sure, but something downright terrifying may be afoot.

Day Seven
Nothing unusual happened with the bears, like always. Oh snap. I've already been in the forest for a week. I feel like I'm starting to forget why I'm here.

Day Eight
That damn snake attacked me again.

This time, we weren't far from my base.

I'm pretty sure I'd originally found it deep in the forest. Did it move its den after it started chasing me? That would mean it's definitely out for blood. I don't want to be eaten.

I should take down the Grand Grizzly soon.

Something doesn't feel right.

Day Nine
The rabbit looked scared in the morning, so we spent the day resting up in the tree. We're on the last droplets of water we'd fetched, but more of it's not worth risking my life. Either way, this rabbit seems to like me a little too much. I know I healed its wounds, but usually that wouldn't make someone feel so . . . attached.

Honestly, I'd love to take it home with me. If the snake doesn't come back tomorrow, then it's time to hunt down that bear.

On the tenth day, I realized that I couldn't take down the Grand Grizzly. It wasn't that my desperate tactics had failed—in fact,

I hadn't put them into action at all. Before I had the chance to go through with my plan, I found the brutally ravaged, half-devoured remains of that very Grand Grizzly.

"Brutal." It perfectly described the battered state of the corpse.

Lying there was the Grand Grizzly that Rose had told me to kill. Its arms and legs were broken and twisted in unnatural directions. In addition, there was a laceration on the corpse that suggested it was bitten by something enormous. The body of a Blue Grizzly was lying next to it in a similar state.

"Downright disturbing."

Something really angered me when I saw the slain monsters. Whatever did this didn't eat them—it just brutally slayed them and left. I wasn't mad because my prey was taken from me, but for a different reason altogether.

"Rose is gonna kill me."

I didn't watch the bears die, but it was obvious that *something* had slaughtered them. There was only one monster in the area that could kill them without a fight, and it was none other than the snake who looked like a tsuchinoko. I had all the proof I needed. There were two bite marks on the Grand Grizzly's neck that looked just like they came from a snake. Even though my target was dead, I couldn't even prove that I'd killed it if I tried.

"Shit . . . shit, shit!"

If I pulled out one of the bear's fangs and brought it to Rose, I could probably trick her into believing I'd killed it. But no one could pull one over on old crazy Rose. She would probably doubt me and learn the truth . . . and if that happened, I'd be suffering a fate worse than death.

I punched a nearby tree out of frustration. I couldn't think straight. Just then, I heard the rabbit cry out. It was sending out a warning.

"Ack! It's here?!"

That damn snake is coming.

I focused all my power into my legs and was ready to escape. Suddenly, a small blue shadow emerged from the brush.

"Grrr . . ." it cried.

I let down my guard. "You're the Blue Grizzly cub, aren't you?"

He was only about one meter tall.

Too upset to pay me any notice, the cub whimpered sadly as it approached the two corpses.

"Grrr . . ." it whimpered.

I didn't know what to say.

I rarely helped people out of compassion, but I also didn't look down on people out of vitriol. Rose could put me through hell and make me decently strong, but even so, that core part of my personality would never change.

No matter how hard I tried, I was still just a high schooler who hated losing.

I hated losing, so I didn't like the idea of losing at the task Rose assigned me. I didn't like that my prey had been stolen from me, and that my decision to employ my tactics had been for nothing. But what I hated most of all . . . was seeing that cub sadly whimper.

I knew it didn't make any sense.

After all, I had set out to hunt the Grand Grizzly myself! Instead, it was killed by the snake, which was probably a direct result of my actions. Even so, I couldn't just ignore the sad scene that was unfolding before me. I knew there was only one way to fix this.

"I'm going to take down the enemy. Wait here," I said to the cub.

Only one thing would satisfy me: killing that snake. No more running away. This time I was going to fight. Filled with determination, I turned away from the cub and headed into the forest.

* * *

Far from Llinger Kingdom was a land that was enshrouded in dark, menacing clouds—a land that was entirely unsuitable for human occupation. In a certain place within the country, a tall, eerie castle pierced the gray sky.

"Hmph," grumbled the lord of the castle.

The lord was an attractive man. He sat in his heavily embellished throne as a tall woman kneeled before him. However, the woman didn't look like—and in fact, wasn't—a typical human. She had dark brown skin and red hair that fell to her shoulders, but she also had two twisted goat horns that stuck out of her head. The man haughtily asked the red-haired woman a question.

"Well? How are the plans to invade Llinger Kingdom coming along?"

"Everything is proceeding smoothly. Our units are swiftly preparing for battle. We should be able to start the advance in the near future." The woman sounded indifferent.

"I see. I'll leave all the commanding to you. Humans these days are a force to be reckoned with. It seems that things have changed. Quite different from the days when those snobs trusted a champion to single-handedly win a war," he remarked.

The lord looked into the distance, as if remembering something long gone, then quickly glanced back at the woman who was still on her knees.

"They may have won by a small margin, but they still drove us out of their land. I won't tell you to fight to the death . . . but I do expect you to give it your all," he urged.

"I will do my utmost to meet your request," she answered.

"Wise decision. If that's all, leave at once," he ordered.

"Understood."

The woman respectfully bowed her head and left the room. She then heaved a great sigh. It was almost as if she was releasing all the stress in her body.

"Ugh. Meeting with the Demon Lord is as pleasant as suffocation," she griped.

"Oh my. Is that something the third army commander should say?" a voice quipped.

"That you, Hyriluk?" she asked.

A man with white ram horns spoke to the grumbling woman.

"Who cares if I complain? The Demon Lord is forgiving. That little cheeky remark wouldn't bother him anyway. So. What's up with you, Demon Doctor?" she queried.

"Quit calling me by that weird nickname, will ya?" he hissed.

"Ugh." The woman started walking away as if she had lost interest in the conversation.

Hyriluk scratched his head nervously. "Ha ha ha . . . to answer your question, I finished the prototype for the first demon-made monster."

"Ooh," she said.

The man grew excited. "It's got strong venom, a large body, sharp fangs, and on top of that, it's got a beautiful—"

"What's its name?" she interrupted.

"Baljinak, Demon-made Monster Prototype Seventy-Two! My greatest creation!" he exclaimed.

"What? Wasn't that the name of prototype seventy-one?" the woman said.

The man fell to his knees and covered his eyes as if he were crying.

"Oh, Baljinak was such a good child. It was driven back the last time we advanced on Llinger Kingdom. After the enemy army commander repelled it, Baljinak was never active again. It was awful! As if my flesh and blood had passed away."

"Army Commander Siglis. He really held his own," the woman remarked.

The image of a knight that was enveloped in smoke floated to the forefront of her mind. He had mowed down his enemies with his unrefined swordsmanship.

"However, his troops weren't our biggest threat," she added.

"Oh. I was at the rear so I wouldn't know. You aren't talking about the 'kidnappers,' are you?" he asked.

"Yeah. They're soldiers that won't fight even though they stand on the battlefield. You have no idea how much hell they gave us when we set foot on their land." The woman winced as she remembered her advance into Llinger Kingdom. The invasion tactic she employed had failed, and it had deeply wounded her pride.

"Well, in that case, why don't you just target them first?" he asked.

"We can't. They're not your average soldiers. Not only are they tough, but they carry injured men off the field at abnormal speeds. Plus, their boss is . . ." she said, trailing off.

"Their boss?" he wondered.

"She's a healer," she stated.

"I see. So, her subordinates bring the injured somewhere safe so she can heal them?" he guessed.

"No, that's her subordinates' job. The boss flings herself into battle and heals her own wounds as she fights. What annoys me the most is that no matter how many times she gets hit, she heals her fatigue in an instant. It's almost like she's immortal. Your run-of-the-mill healer could never recover that fast. That hidden rare strain of magic keeps her body in tip-top shape," she explained.

"Normal human bodies can't withstand such magic," he stated.

The man wasn't called a "demon doctor" for nothing.

The man had his fair share of human test subjects, so he knew a great deal about their bodies and limitations. Even if one were to manifest multiple superhuman abilities, a normal human being couldn't handle the pain it would cause to their muscles, their bones, and their organs. Anyone who would push their body to such limits was nothing more than an ill-advised fool.

"The problem is that she gets through it due to her unyielding persistence. Before the Demon Lord was resurrected, she won a deadly duel against my master. All she lost in that fight was her right eye. She's a full-blown monstrosity," the woman muttered.

"A duel with the first army commander? She *must* be a monster," he agreed.

The woman's master was said to be as strong as the entire demon race itself. Anyone who survived that duel was no average human.

"**And** she survived? Sounds rather skilled," he observed.

"The new troops didn't believe me when I told them, but I'm sure they'll change their minds after we advance and she tortures them." Her words dripped with hate.

"Oof. Sounds brutal," he said weakly.

"This time, I'll avenge my master. I'll make sure that she—that Rose—is defeated."

Hyriluk then mentioned that her master was still alive, but she ignored him as she looked toward Llinger Kingdom.

"I, Amila Vergrett, will get my revenge!" she exclaimed.

"You're a commander this time, so you're not allowed to go to the front lines," he reminded her.

"Oh," she remembered. "That's right . . ."

*   *   *

I told the Blue Grizzly cub that I'd hunt down that devious snake, so I spent the night making a simple spear out of a nearby branch. I sharpened it with my knife as I sat up in the tree. Naturally, I had no idea whether this slapdash weapon would work. I didn't know how to set traps. On top of that, the only weapon-like items I had were my magic and the knife. But that was all the more reason to have at least one trick up my sleeve.

"Yep. All done."

It was nothing more than a stick, but it was still sharp. After I put the spear in a safe spot nearby, I leaned back against the tree. I had already gotten used to sleeping on that hard branch every night.

"I wonder what Kazuki and Inukami-senpai are up to," I murmured.

"Kyu?" The rabbit seemed curious.

"You stuck by me all this time," I said. The rabbit gazed up at me as I patted its head. It was quite a strange creature, but I wouldn't have survived in the forest without it.

"There might be trouble tomorrow. I hope that's all right."

The rabbit nodded in response.

Satisfied by its answer, I slowly drifted to sleep.

The next day, I used the rabbit as a radar to search for the snake. I only had my knife and my spear—I'd left everything else back in the tree. Naturally, I had also taken a bath to wash off my scent. I was all ready to go. I was ready to find the snake . . . but then I saw the rabbit tremble.

"What's wrong?"

It was staring straight ahead. I gripped the spear tight as my hand started to sweat. Proceeding with as much caution as possible, I silently pushed through the brush.

"Is that the sound of a fight?" I whispered.

I heard something. Something terribly loud. It was such an earsplitting sound that I thought the trees were being chopped down. But even so, I slowly made my way through the brush as I gazed straight ahead.

I saw my target: the snake.

But the Blue Grizzly cub was there too.

"It's him!" I said, surprised.

The cub had bruises all over his body. He was past the point of exhaustion but still breathing. I placed the rabbit on the ground and grabbed my spear with both hands.

"Stay back."

I knew what had to be done. I was prepared. Not prepared to die, but to punish the snake for picking on someone much weaker than him.

"It's go time!"

The snake was nowhere near as intimidating as Rose. I knew how scary that savage, cold-blooded hag could be. This was nothing in comparison.

"You don't scare me!" I shouted, surprising the cub and the snake.

For a split second, the snake didn't know who to attack.

Now's my chance! I know I'm much smaller, but I should strike while it's thinking so I can get the upper hand. The thing is there's no way my spear can pierce the giant scales that protect it.

So, what do I do? I'll strike. There's only one place to attack.

"Graaah!" I shouted.

I took one giant step toward the snake. It was far bigger up close. Its teeth were enormous! One bite would surely kill me.

Hm? The path ahead is all dark.

"Bwuh?!" I babbled. I took a giant step back.

Its mouth had snapped closed right in front of my eyes. If I hadn't jumped back, I would have been snake food. But this was the moment I'd been waiting for. The tables had turned, and I raised my spear above my head.

"Eat this, you silly-ass snake!" I shouted gruffly without even thinking.

At that moment I brandished my spear and jammed it into the snake's right eye. I was ready to shove my spear all the way to its core.

"Gyaaaaaaaaaah!" I screamed.

I focused all my power into my arm.

"What the—?! Huh?!"

As I tightened my grip on the spear, a terrifying impact

jolted my body and sent me flying back through the air. I enveloped myself in healing magic out of instinct. My back slammed hard against a tree. I stared down the snake as I staggered back to my feet.

"Nrgh. The damn tail."

I'm an idiot. Of course, this strange snake's gonna fight with its tail.

Even so, the snake had just lost an eye. Its attacks were nothing compared to the blow I had landed. After I healed all my wounds, I wielded the knife.

"Is that it?! I didn't feel a thing!"

I aimed for the right side of its body. The snake came charging at me, so I tried running into its blind spot. I knew that if it lashed out at full power, dodging it would be easy. I entered its blind spot as expected . . . but then it suddenly froze and faced me.

"Huh?!"

I'd been naïve. I'd assumed it was a wild animal that was simply going berserk, but that wasn't the case. This snake was different. It thought before it acted, before it slaughtered, and before it went in for the kill. In other words, this snake . . . was enjoying messing with me.

The snake opened its mouth wide and sunk its fangs into my left shoulder.

"Nrgh. Graaaaaaah!" I shrieked.

Ow, ow, ow, ow, ow, YEOWCH!

The fangs sunk even deeper. I screamed out in agony, but it wasn't trying to rip off my shoulder. It was looking at me with the round-eyed stare that was unique to cold-blooded creatures.

"Heh heh." I had found my way out.

I held the knife in my left hand and thrust it into the roof of its mouth. It was the only part of the snake that wasn't covered in scales. I stuck my right hand between my left shoulder and its bottom teeth, using as much force as I could.

"Graaah!"

"Ssssssss!"

The snake tried to force its mouth shut. It refused to let go.

But ever since I came to this world, I'd been put through hellish training.

When it came to strength, let's just say I was a little bit confident.

Actually, no. I can't do this. I could do it if I had both my arms, but with just one there's no way. At this rate, I'll have to say goodbye to my left arm forever!

I couldn't feel my left arm anymore. I kept pouring healing magic into it, but I couldn't replace all the blood I had lost.

"Hm? Left . . . hand? That's it!"

I twisted the knife into the roof of the snake's mouth.

I was hoping it would cause it great pain. As expected, the snake loosened its grip.

"Take this!"

I saw my opening, pried the snake's mouth open, and withdrew my left hand. Then I took a step back and gripped my arm. It was dripping with blood. The snake writhed in the pain that ran through its mouth. It was another chance to attack, but my knife was stuck in its mouth. I had lost all my weapons, but I still had hope.

"**That's** the only target left."

My target was the ugly head it had raised into the air. Unwilling to give it time to heal, I quickly ran toward it.

"Huh?"

My vision blurred and I felt all the power in my arms and legs fade away. I administered first aid, but I knew there was only one thing that could cause this.

"Poison? You gotta be kidding me."

Not only is it huge, but it's poisonous?! That's just plain unfair.

The odds were against me, but this was my last chance to strike and I wasn't about to let it escape. A little poison wouldn't slow me down!

I enveloped my entire body in all the magic I had.

If poison is eating away at me, internal healing should do the trick.

Excruciating pain rushed through my body as I kicked off the ground and started running.

"Graaaaaaaah!" I shouted.

The snake noticed me charging toward it and tried to hit me with its tail. I couldn't evade its attack, but that didn't matter.

If it hit me, I'd simply heal. Right before the tail hit me, a blue figure jumped in the way.

"Grrrrr!" growled something cute.

"It's you!" I exclaimed.

The Blue Grizzly cub . . . did he just save my life?

The cub glanced at me for a second before it let out a shriek of pain, and then pinned down the snake's tail. After exchanging glances with the cub, I silently turned to the snake.

Its head was higher up than I could reach, so the only option I had was to scale the giant snake's body. It rampaged wildly as it tried to shake me off. I was almost thrown off, but I stubbornly held on as tight as I could.

I finally reached the snake's head. It was shaking more violently than ever.

"If you think you can shake me off . . . then think again, dumbass!"

I held on to one of its scales and dug my heels into both sides of its head. Now it couldn't shake me so easily! After that, I let go of its scale and swung my fist above its head.

"Calm the hell down!"

I punched the top of its head as it struggled against me. Its scales reduced the efficacy of my attack, but I figured I was still powerful enough to at least make it flinch. My fist hit its head with a *clang*. The snake quivered and swayed as it fell to the ground. While the snake was still disoriented, I jumped down from its head and grabbed the spear in its eye with my right hand.

"Say goodnight!"

I focused all my power into my right arm and sunk the spear deeper into its eye. The snake was still trying to shake me off, so I pushed the spear even deeper. Suddenly, it stopped moving and fell to the ground with a *thud*.

The snake had flung me to the ground, and I was now lying outstretched on my back. As I lay there, I glanced at the snake out of the corner of my eye.

"Ha ha ha . . . I did it!" I yelled.

"Grrr," the Blue Grizzly growled.

The Blue Grizzly was close by. Bruised from head to toe, it came walking toward me. I thought it was going to eat me, but then I realized that it didn't see me as an enemy. The cub planted itself beside me and whimpered as it stared into my eyes.

"I took down the snake."

"Grrr," the cub said.

What's this bear cub going to do after this? Can it really survive in this forest? No, I shouldn't be worried. I mean, it fought that snake for crying out loud. If it's got that much courage, it should be all right.

"Ksha . . . sha . . ."

I heard a dreadful cry. I'd thought the fight was over, but I was dead wrong.

"Nrh?! No way!"

The snake slowly picked itself up. Its eyes were dripping with hate.

"Grrr . . . Grr . . ." the cub growled.

"C'mon, we gotta run. Let's go!" I shouted.

The bear cub bit into my clothes and tried to drag me away. I couldn't move and felt frustratingly helpless. I started crying, convinced this was the end.

Kazuki, Inukami-senpai, Rose . . .

That's right. All of this is Rose's fault. I should be allowed to curse her name if I'm doing it with my very last breath.

"Damn thuuuug! Old haaaaag! Freaking shrewww! Stupid ooooogre!"

The snake opened its mouth and charged us.

Rose you damn devil! Even if I die, I'm gonna curse you from hell!

The moment I should have died in that wide open mouth, **something** had vanquished the snake.

"Huh?" I couldn't believe it.

"Tch. Nothing but a rotten pile of trash. Should've just died without makin' a scene."

And there appeared a woman with green hair raising her foot from the crushed head of the snake. On her shoulder was the black rabbit I had grown to know so well.

The bear cub and I stood there with our jaws dropped to the ground. It took a few seconds for me to grasp what had happened, but when I did my whole body trembled. Naturally, I was terrified.

"Yo. Nice work, Usato."

"R-Rose-sama?!"

I'd added "-sama" to her name without even thinking.

But I suppose it's only natural to use "-sama" when confronted with a tyrant.

She watched me tremble with fear, then petted the black rabbit and grinned.

"If it hadn't been for this little fella, you woulda been toast," she remarked.

"That rabbit . . ." I trailed off.

"Huh? Rabbit? What the hell're you talking about? This ain't no ordinary rabbit, you know. It's my pet. Name's Kukuru. It's been watching over you 'cause I told it to," Rose said.

What was once my guardian angel now turned out to be my worst enemy.

"See, I was standin' on the outskirts of the forest in case something went wrong . . . but I never would've thought one of the monsters from the invasion would have escaped into the forest after Siglis had wounded it. Anyway, I tried to stay out of yer hair as much as I could," Rose said.

"Invasion? By the Demon Lord's army?" I asked.

Did she really watch that damn snake chase me around? I don't know what to say anymore. I'm already used to this brute.

"But y'see, I never expected it to kill the Grand Grizzly. The Grand Grizzly is supposed to be the toughest monster in the forest."

"What?! Are you telling me that you wanted my first fight to be with the king of the forest?!"

How callous! How cruel!!

"No. You got it all wrong. Normally, you can't kill it. You'd lose yer life if you fought it on the first day, so I was gonna have you fight high-ranking enemies and gain experience. I was gonna pit you against the Grizzly on the tenth day until . . ." Rose trailed off.

"Until what?" I asked.

"Until I saw ya doin' cool shit! I wanted to see what you'd do so I just let it play out," she added.

"But I almost died!" I exclaimed.

Are you serious? So, everything I did to survive was only going to kill me in the end?

I felt totally deflated. Rose started approaching, but I didn't care what she was going to do to me anymore.

"Grrr!"

The Blue Grizzly club jumped between me and Rose.

This isn't good. Don't cross that woman. She's much eviler than the snake! Really!

"Hm? You the Blue Grizzly's cub? You like the rookie or somethin'?" Rose asked.

"What? He likes me?" I said, befuddled.

I'd felt I had a bond with the cub. Is it possible that it felt that way too?

"Hah! Looks like you and I got somethin' in common, cub. Get over here."

Rose called out to the bear cub, who trembled at the sound of her voice.

I guess monsters really do wince when they meet Rose, what with her being so much more powerful and all.

"You're coming with us. Carry this escape artist outta here," she commanded.

"Bwuh? What the hell are you talking about? Can we really bring a monster back to the kingdom?!" I asked.

"Just who do you think I am? I'll make them okay with it. Got it?" she said gruffly.

Yikes. She's way too aggressive.

"Plus, I was plannin' on bringing Kukuru back with me. Doesn't matter if others wanna tag along," she added.

That doesn't make any damn sense! We don't even know if this cub is actually gonna follow us. Wait, what? Why is the Blue Grizzly picking me up?!

"Grrr."

"Huh? You wanna come with us? Are you sure you don't want to stay in the forest where your parents grew up?" I asked.

The bear cub started swaying in response, almost as if

it understood what I was asking by intuition alone. The cub seemed to feel indebted to me.

I heaved a sigh and asked Rose a question that had been on my mind.

"How was the rabbit injured?"

"Huh? That was just to throw you off. It was all an act," she answered.

"Kyu," the rabbit said.

Don't look so proud of yourself, Mr. Rabbit! Seeing you hurt like that practically tore me to pieces. Now I know why it understands what I say. This was all part of Rose's plan. I just wanna cry.

"Welp, for now let's take the kid somewhere safe," Rose said.

She grunted as she picked up the bear cub I was riding.

Ugh. This lady scares me.

"By the way . . ." Rose started.

Tears were welling up in my eyes as Rose turned to me with a smile. A blue vein was jutting out of her forehead.

"Remind me. What did you just call me? A damn thug? An old hag? A freaking shrew? A stupid ogre? I'm only twenty-five years old, ya know. When we get home prepare yourself for a beating."

That was when it hit me.

I realized that my greatest enemy wasn't the snake.

"So, if I round up, that makes you thirty."

"Good luck sleepin' tonight."

My greatest enemy had always been this terrifying captain.

*　　*　　*

We finally returned to Llinger Kingdom.

Rose used her magic to treat the venom and wounds. Even though I'd only spent ten days holed up in the forest, coming back to Llinger Kingdom made me realize just how long it had felt. Only ten days had passed, but they were jam-packed with adventure.

I brought the Blue Grizzly cub—who I had affectionately named Blurin—to an old stable close to the rescue team's living quarters and healed all its wounds.

Its blue fur felt pleasant to the touch.

"Heh, it's a pretty good name if I do say so myself. Don't you agree, Blurin?"

Yeah, "Blurin" is a really good name. Just take the "Blu" from "Blue" and "Ri" from "Grizzly" and bam! You've got a name fit for an adorable mascot.

I put my hand on his head, which he bit with a *homf.* It seemed as though he agreed. He looked happy to have been given a name.

Ha ha ha. That's enough play biting—you know, now that I'm bleeding and everything.

Even though Blurin's teeth wouldn't part from my hand, we somehow received permission to bring him into the country. I honestly thought that they might turn him away, but Rose told me that so long as they obey humans, and so long as we can guarantee they won't cause too much trouble, monsters like Rose's rabbit Kukuru were allowed to stay in the kingdom after a few days of observation.

Having monsters in the kingdom required complicated paperwork, but Rose said she would take care of that for me.

Was she sweet or was she scary? I really didn't know.

"Now here's the deal," I started.

"Kyu?" Kukuru looked flustered.

"Yes, you. You're a turncoat . . . or shall I say turn-**hare**?"

I wasn't mincing words.

"Kyuu!" the rabbit exclaimed.

"So cute. But playing dumb and cute like that won't get you out of this," I said.

Rose's pet rabbit Kukuru had followed me and Blurin to the stable. It was a member of the Noir Rabbit species. Rose had told me that this species was fairly rare . . . but even so, this rabbit had a criminal history.

He was guilty of toying with my pure, naive heart! He once acted hurt to get close to me! I would've admired him for the almost-too-courageous facade he put on for his master . . . if it wasn't used to trick me, that is.

"Nope, I just can't get over it. If Rose had a pet, I'd have thought it'd be a dragon or a perilous legendary beast . . . but no! You're cute! How freaking deceitful!" I shouted.

"Gwah!" Blurin bit me.

"Yeowch! Sorry!" I apologized.

*You're **both** cute, Blurin! Okay? So no more punching my shins!*

Kukuru looked bewildered, watching as I desperately tried enduring the pain. It watched me turn away, then yelped before jumping onto something else.

When I turned around, Kukuru was standing on Rose's shoulder.

"That's a good boy," she cooed.

"Rose-san," I said, surprised.

"'Sup. Just cleared all the paperwork. That bear is now property of the rescue team," she stated.

"P-Property?" I stuttered.

Well, I guess it made sense. After all, the team wasn't renting the stable for free, plus we had to think about feeding the cub. This bear was going to have to work to earn its keep. Knowing this, I glanced over at Blurin, who had thrust his head into a pile of hay.

Blurin . . . I know Rose is scary, but that's just overreacting.

"Welp, that about wraps it up for the bear. I came here to talk about that hulking pile of waste," she said.

Pile of waste? Is she talking about the snake?

"The rabb—I mean . . . Kukuru brought me to clean water. That was when we ran into the snake, when we were deep in the forest," I explained.

"Gotcha. Sounds like it healed itself and gathered power where we couldn't find it. But to think it'd kill a Grand Grizzly . . ." Rose trailed off.

"Um . . ." I started.

"What?" she asked.

"How dangerous would you say that Grand Grizzly was?"

I simply wanted to know how much danger she had literally thrown me into.

Looking annoyed, Rose folded her arms. "Well . . . a squadron of our most elite troops couldn't kill it. How's that? In terms of strength, maybe slightly weaker than commander Siglis? Dangerous enough to be at the top of the forest's food chain."

"Are you insane?!" I blurted out.

"Pardon?" Rose said menacingly.

"Sorry, ma'am." I apologized immediately even though I was letting my enemy win.

Wait a sec. A squadron of our country's most elite troops couldn't kill the Grand Grizzly, and here I was holding my own against it. I don't want to toot my own horn or anything, but I did a pretty good job!

I casually mentioned that I thought I did okay. Surprisingly, she didn't criticize me or put me down.

"As for the trial? You pass. Actually, you aced it. You didn't kill your target, but you brought that pile of trash to its knees. You qualify," she stated.

"Qualify for what?" I asked.

"Qualify to fight on the same battlefield as me. You still need to master the basics, but you're different from the other healers. You got somethin' they just don't have," she mentioned.

"I'm different? How?"

"You can handle excruciating pain and your physical abilities are off the charts. Not to mention . . ." Rose said, suddenly putting her fist to my chest, "your heart is as strong as your mind. The other healers aren't like that. You should be proud."

"Heh. It doesn't really feel like it but . . . wait. What happened to the other healers?" I asked. Since I still hadn't met them, I had forgotten that there were two other healers on the rescue team.

"One of them is frail. The other one's his younger sister. They run an infirmary in the castle town together," Rose explained.

"I see. So that means . . ." I trailed off.

I felt incredibly jealous at that moment.

Those two healers probably didn't have to go through all this training!

"They're backup in case of emergencies. Tong and the others transport the injured. You and I heal 'em on the front lines," Rose stated.

"On the front lines?!" I repeated.

"Well, yeah. Since you're the same as me," Rose said.

"But . . . why?" I asked.

"There's no time. The Demon Lord's army'll be here any day now. Odds are they won't repeat their previous blunders, meaning they'll take me down as soon as they can. That's where you—our secret weapon—show 'em who's boss."

Was she saying that I was the trump card against the Demon Lord's army? No, that'd be giving me way too much credit. Maybe I was more like the pawn that would trick the opponent into exposing its weakness.

Can I really do something so important? Will I be able to stay calm on the battlefield, in a fight of life or death?

"Worrying ain't gonna help. But you need to steel yerself, got it? There's gonna be heroes on the battlefield," Rose remarked.

"You don't mean . . .!" I said.

Kazuki and Inukami.

As heroes, it was only natural that they would fight the Demon Lord's army.

What do I do? To be honest, I don't want to fight a war. But the bigger issue is that I want to save my friends.

Maybe it was my stubbornness or my sense of pride talking, but it felt wrong for me to simply do nothing when we were all in the same mess. They were trying their hardest, so taking cover on the sidelines wasn't an option. We weren't super close back on Earth, but in the end the two of them had become extremely important to me.

Deep down, I already knew what I was going to do.

I knew I might die when I was fighting the snake. Hearing the story of the Demon Lord's army made me cherish my friends more now than ever. I wasn't the same person I was back on Earth—the boy who avoided all risks like the plague. This world, this country . . . this **place** had turned my entire life around.

I didn't know how much I had changed. But what I did know was that I had become friends with Inukami and Kazuki, that I belonged on the rescue team, and that I had grown stronger by enduring training that made me hurl blood.

That was why . . .

"I will not fight," I stated.

"Oh?" Rose looked amused.

Strength comes in many forms. Inukami and Kazuki were the heroes in Llinger Kingdom that would fend off the invasion from the Demon Lord's army. I, on the other hand, was going to fight how I pleased.

"I will not kill my enemies," I added.

"Oh?" Rose repeated.

I didn't need swords or other weapons to kill my enemies.

"But I **will** save as many people as possible. Otherwise, I wouldn't be a member of the rescue team," I said.

I was ready—ready to stand with Rose and protect this country as a member of the rescue team. I would use healing magic to save the country that had taken me in when I was merely sent here by accident, and to save the two friends I held dear.

"Good. We're the rescue team. No need to kill the enemy. It's all about rescuing people. For those who want to be martyrs, just knock 'em out and drag 'em off the battlefield. Whisk away soldiers from the clutches of death. If someone dies, revive 'em. That is our role on the battlefield. You get all that, rookie? Speak your ideals and keep 'em comin'. That's what the rescue team's all about." Rose flashed a fierce smile, and I instinctively straightened my posture.

My path was clear. I stared into her left eye and answered, "Yes, Captain!"

That was the first time I truly felt like a member of the rescue team.

CHAPTER 4

Usato Makes the Most of His Life!

Even after I told Rose that I'd dedicate myself to the rescue team, I still ended up getting in trouble. She was apparently still angry that I'd called her all those bad names, which was why she locked me in a room and put me through weight-training hell. My memories of last night weren't exactly all intact. I could only assume that I was worked to the bone.

The next thing I knew, I woke up in my bed.

"W-What did she do to me?" I muttered to myself.

I heard a voice. "Mornin' Usato," it said.

"Is that you, Tong?" I replied to my roommate as I climbed out of bed. "Haven't seen you in a while."

Seeing his ugly mug would make any grown man run for his life. This was pretty much the epitome of waking up on the wrong side of the bed.

I got dressed while I made small talk with Tong, washed down breakfast—a piece of rock-hard bread—with some milk, then I stepped outside the quarters. I borrowed a bucket from the dining hall and filled it with fruit on the way to the small stable.

"You awake, Blurin?" I asked.

The bear replied with a "Grrr?"

He had just woken up. I patted the sleepy cub and took out

a piece of fruit from the bucket. His nose inched toward the fruit, sniffing around for its scent. Then, he opened his mouth wide and filled his cheeks.

"Good boy," I said.

He munched away.

After slowly chewing and swallowing his food, I gave him one more piece of fruit and continued petting him with my other hand.

Hee hee. Look at him being all quiet. His fur feels so nice.

If anyone had seen me grinning like that, they probably would've thought that I was a creep. To be frank, I just didn't care. People could say what they want. This was my first time having a pet and I loved it.

"Tch. There you are," said a gruff voice. "I wasted my damn time looking for you." Rose slunk into the entrance with an irritated look on her face. She was *always* irritated, so I didn't think anything of it.

"Ro—. . . Captain? Is everything okay?" I asked. "Training's not until later."

"Today's training involves him," she grunted. "What's his name?"

"You mean Blurin?" I asked.

She looked surprised. "Blu. . . rin? Is that *really* his name?"

Rose's eyes widened; they were as wide and round as glass plates. She almost never made this face, so I found it somewhat refreshing.

"You don't mind that weird-ass name?" she asked the bear.

"Huh? It's a plenty good name! Right, Blurin?" I protested.

Why would she say that? His name is amazing! She's just being rude. You think so, too, dontcha Blurin?

I went to pet Blurin's head when it nipped my hand with a *homf.*

Heh. He must be feeling bashful. These are just love bites, so I don't mind them at all.

"See? Blurin likes it just fine," I stated.

"Well, whatever," Rose said. "Anyway, Blurin's gonna train with you starting today."

Me and Blurin?

He stopped gnawing on my hand and tilted his head as he looked up at Rose.

"This cub's a member of the rescue team now. He's gonna be your training partner," she noted.

"Hmm. Wanna train, Blurin?" I asked the cub.

Blurin cried out as if he were cheering himself on.

"Looks like he's ready," I said.

"We've wasted enough time. Let's move," Rose instructed.

Blurin and I walked out of the stable with Rose. For some reason, my heart leaped when I thought about resuming my intensive training.

Wait. Has she got me trained like some animal?

"Now, put Blurin on your back and start runnin'," she commanded.

"Come again?" I asked, dazed.

I had no idea what she meant.

Why do I have to put him on my back? I thought me and the cub were supposed to run together.

"Watch your mouth," she threatened. "You're gonna carry weights and the bear when you run."

"Weights too?!" I exclaimed.

"No shit. That bear's heavier than an average person, so it works. This training'll simulate an actual battle. Pretend he's a wounded soldier and run for your life. No cuttin' corners either. I want you to act like you're on the battlefield," Rose instructed.

"Okay. . ." I answered. I didn't have much of a choice.

I put on something that looked like a weighted vest and loaded Blurin onto my back. The heavy weight of the vest felt kind of nostalgic. It was almost as if I was reuniting with an old friend.

This'll be easy. I got this.

"You okay, Blurin?" I asked.

"Gwah," he replied, lightly smacking the back of my head.

The touch of Blurin's little paws filled me with motivation. Rose took a seat in the shade of a nearby tree and started reading a slightly dense-looking book. I started laughing under my breath.

"I'll show you what a killer combo Blurin and I make, Captain!" I called out.

"Shut up already and go," she said, clearly irritated.

In an attempt to avoid Rose's wrath, I leaned forward and started running on the course she had set. I was to run through the small patch of woods that surrounded the training area, which left me essentially running in circles.

One thing I noticed was that I was light on my feet. My bones and my muscles had gotten stronger, too, though I didn't know if it was because I'd survived the forest, or if it was from all that rapid healing I'd used when fighting the snake. I couldn't be sure.

"This shouldn't be possible. This isn't a manga after all," I mumbled.

"Grrr?" The cub looked confused.

"Oh, sorry. Was just talking to myself," I answered.

While I was running, I covered my body in a veil of gentle green healing magic. The magic was much more effective when it was focused, but its power still healed every inch of my body. Without this magic, keeping up with Rose's training wouldn't be possible.

Two hours had passed since I'd started my training. I was running at a fixed pace but still wasn't tired, and I had managed to use less magic than needed. I realized that if I quit over an easy exercise like this, I simply didn't have a future on the rescue team.

"I can keep going," I said to myself.

But right after I hit the four-hour mark, I started feeling strange. My legs felt as heavy as lead, and I found it nearly impossible to breathe. I had more than enough energy to keep going, but something unknown was slowing me down.

Blurin swayed nervously on my back, but my body refused to respond. I grew heavier still and my speed slowed down significantly. Just as the sun was crossing its highest point in the sky, I stumbled. I helped Blurin to the ground, then I lay flat on my back with my arms and legs spread out in exhaustion. I tried catching my breath.

"What is this feeling?" I asked myself.

"Yo, kid! What's the hold up? You can't rescue people if you're taking it easy!" Rose called out. I was too tired to say anything back.

Apparently, my magic had completely ran out. I usually didn't run out of magic for half a day at least, but today was an exception. While I lay there on the ground, Rose stopped reading her book in the shade to come scold me.

"Get it now? That's how long yer body will last if we assume you've got a guy on your back," she said, still glaring at me.

"Why. . . assume that?" I inquired.

"Well, the body's a funny thing. Stress changes just how tired you get. Even feelings like anxiety, fear, and irritation can wear you down. If we assume that a soldier's gonna take Blurin's place, you won't have as much energy on the battlefield as you do now."

"So, what should I do?" I asked.

"Get used to this training. You've gotta learn how to make good decisions. Keep your head above water and stare fear in the face. You'll be training like this from now on. Capiche?" she said, putting the green light that shone from her palm to my head.

The moment that warm light surrounded me, I felt my fatigue escape from my body. This didn't restore my magic power, of course, but I was at least healed to the point where I could get back on my feet.

"Thank you very much," I said.

"Focus on restoring your magic. You're gonna do the same training tonight," she stated.

No matter how rough she was, she really looked out for her team. I knew this because she didn't go back to town; she stayed here with me in the forest. She was also fond of animals, which definitely caught me off guard.

"Captain, you're such a—" I started.

"Huh?" she asked.

"—tsundere," I said.

"The hell does that even mean?" she hissed.

She would've killed me if she knew what it meant, so I

decided to lock the word away in my chest. "Never mind. It's nothing," I said.

"Good. Tonight, you're runnin' in town and outside the castle," she ordered.

"Wuh?" I was dumbfounded.

She was truly one of a kind.

*   *   *

As part of my training, I visited the castle town for the second time.

According to Rose, my mission was to run at a slower speed to avoid bumping into civilians. In other words, I had to get used to running through crowds. However, that was made slightly more difficult because I stood out like a sore thumb—especially since I had a huge blue bear on my back. I thought Blurin would scare the townspeople, what with him being a monster and all, but instead they glanced at me with tired eyes that looked like they were saying, "This again?"

"Why aren't people making a scene, Blurin?" I asked semi-rhetorically.

I was a boy who was wearing a strange vest over my training uniform while carrying a giant bear on my back. If I were them, I would've definitely called the police.

"Maybe it's good they're not panicking. Makes it easier to focus," I noted.

The castle town was fairly large. I had only been there once before and didn't know it too well, yet here I was, not running in a back alley, but on a main road that was teeming with people. The good thing was that if I were to get lost, I knew I could use the big castle as my compass.

To my surprise, there were many stalls on the street. In fact, I even saw a stall that sold the same fruit I had given to Blurin that morning.

Must be a specialty in this country. I'll ask Tong about it later.

"Heyyy!" someone said. But I figured they weren't talking to me.

Delicious scents wafted through the air, which was something I hadn't noticed on my last visit. I ran as I gazed at the stores that lined the streets, admiring the abundance of unique foods that didn't exist back on Earth.

"Haah, haah . . . wait up!" cried the same voice I'd heard a moment ago.

Wait a second. What's that? It was closer a second ago, but now it's farther away. Maybe that person's talking to me.

When I turned around, I found a gaunt, exhausted-looking man collapsed on the ground. He was coughing and wheezing about ten meters behind me.

"Wait! Yes, you . . . over here!" he gasped.

I was so confused that I blanked out for a second, but then I immediately snapped back to reality and approached the man who was lying face down in front of me. I put down Blurin for a moment, touched the man's back, and poured healing magic into his body.

"A-Are you all right?" I asked.

The man coughed once more. "You finally . . . noticed me . . ."

It was clear that he wanted to talk to me for some reason. I enveloped him in healing magic as I helped him to his feet. When he stood up, his face was as white as a ghost, looking incredibly sorry for the trouble he'd caused.

The man had striking blond hair and was remarkably handsome. However, I couldn't help but pity him when I noticed the dark bags that hung under his eyes and the dirt that was stuck to his face. The man still looked unwell, so I escorted him to the side of the road and had him sit on a wooden crate that was left unattended.

"How are you feeling?" I asked.

"Sorry about that. And thanks . . ." he said, bashfully scratching his head. His face was a lot brighter now that he had calmed down.

"No need to thank me. Do you have business with me, sir?" I inquired.

"Nah, I just wanted to introduce myself since you're my junior and all. I started chasing after you before I even knew what I was doing," he explained.

I was confused. "Your . . . junior?" I asked.

"Wait. The captain didn't tell you?" he asked in return.

His junior? The only guys in this world who'd have seniority over me would be Tong and the guys, but they're not healers like me so that doesn't count. Oh, wait!

"You must be one of the healers!" I said, glad to have figured it out.

"Looks like the captain didn't really tell you who we are. Well in that case, let's start over. Hi, I'm Orga Fleur and I'm twenty-three years old. You can call me Orga," he said.

"My name is Usato and I recently joined the rescue team. It's nice to meet you, Orga-san," I responded.

The man was a healer like me! Rose had told me about him—that he provided support from the rear, not on the front lines like us.

"Sorry for interrupting your training. I was on my way to pick up some medicine when I saw you carrying a Blue Grizzly. I figured you were a new member, so I thought I'd say hi," he said.

"Really? How did you know I was on the rescue team?" I asked.

Orga chuckled. "Your clothes gave you away. That's a special uniform exclusive to rescue team members."

"Oh, wow. I had no idea! I'd just assumed it was regular sportswear or something," I remarked.

"Well, it's also because Tong and the guys usually run around here. The townsfolk see them train fairly often," he explained.

"I see. So that's why no one was fazed when I started running through town with Blurin," I concluded.

"I can't speak for the others, but seeing that cub sure surprised me," he laughed.

The townspeople were so used to seeing the team's rowdy members running through town that carrying a bear on my back didn't intimidate them. After hearing Orga's explanation, everything started making sense. Blurin looked up at me curiously as I patted him on the head. He then fixed his gaze upon Orga.

"But still, I can't believe there's someone who can finally handle the captain's intense training. We couldn't keep up by a long shot," Orga said with a friendly smile.

"Honestly, I almost didn't make it either. By the way, when you say 'we,' does that include the other healer?" I asked.

"Yeah, the other healer's my sister. She's five years younger than me. We run an infirmary in town together to improve our magic instead of training for physical strength," he explained.

I wondered if family members had similar magic aptitudes, but there was no way I could know. In any case, the rescue team seemed to split into two factions: Tong and the guys were focused on strength while Orga and his sister were focused on magic. On the other hand, Rose and I were the only ones who were focused on both.

"But we're still members of the rescue team. In emergencies, my sister and I heal the wounded at the captain's behest," he explained.

The rescue team really was prepared for the worst. Even so, something struck me as odd. If Orga was a healer like me, why didn't he heal himself when he chased me? Couldn't all healers cure fatigue?

"Are you unable to heal yourself, Orga?" I asked, genuinely curious.

"Oh, that. As much as I'd hate to admit it, I'm not very good at healing myself. I'm much better at healing other people. Plus, I couldn't keep up with the captain's training because my body is weaker than my peers'. That caused a lot of trouble for my sister. I feel pretty bad about it," he admitted.

"Sorry to hear that," I said.

It sounded like the ability to heal varied from person to person.

I think I'll visit their infirmary when I have some free time. I'd love to see what it's like.

"Well, I really should get back to training. You should rest a little more, Orga-san," I said as I stood and put Blurin on my back.

"Sorry to bother you, Usato-kun," he said sullenly.

"Not at all. I'm glad we got to talk," I replied.

I didn't want to rest too much after that, and it wasn't because Rose would be mad at me, but because I wanted to take my training seriously.

"Oh, one more thing," Orga said.

I turned back to look at him. "Yeah?"

Where his once-friendly smile had been was now a solemn frown.

"The captain is . . . No, I just don't want you to hate Rose-san too much. I know she's unhinged . . . but she's much more than that. I wouldn't say she's warm and cuddly, but she's really just awkward, so please . . ."

He was calling her "Rose-san" instead of "Captain," which most likely meant that he was talking about her as a person, not his superior.

"Don't worry. I never hated her in the first place!" I said.

The captain was strict, gruff, and even cruel, but for some reason I couldn't bring myself to hate her. It really bothered me when she threw me into the forest, but if it hadn't been for her, I would have never met Blurin. Everything had turned out all right, so I wasn't going to hold it against her.

More importantly, she was the one who showed me which path I should take in this world. As much as I liked to complain, life with the rescue team wasn't so bad.

Next, I'll run a lap around the castle. Kazuki and senpai should be there at this hour. It's been a while since I've seen them. It'd be nice to catch up. But . . . I don't think I should bring Blurin into the castle. That sounds like nothing but trouble.

*   *   *

I let my mind wander as I watched the boy with a Blue Grizzly cub run to the castle.

"He's the same type of healer as the captain, but I didn't think he'd be so young," I said to myself.

He was quite the balanced healer, whereas my talents were lopsided. In fact, his magic healed me so well that I would say it was perfect. But to think he was still in his twenties . . . I couldn't help but be a little impressed. I looked up at the sky as I sat on the wooden crate he'd brought me to earlier.

"You've finally found one, Rose-san. This time, you won't have to brave the battle alone," I murmured.

"Big brother, how dare you!" a voice exclaimed.

Now that my sister had found me, she started nagging me about how worried she'd been. She looked absolutely distraught (even though there was no need to be). When it came to her "big brother," she just couldn't help it.

"Big brother!! You went outside alone?! Are you TRYING to die?!" she yelled.

"I'm not that weak, okay?" I said, defending myself.

"What? Yes, you are. I'm your sister. I'd know," she stated.

How mean! Well, whatever. I'll let it slide for now. First, I should tell my adorable little sister about the boy I met earlier.

"Anyway, I've got news. Today I met someone very interesting," I mentioned.

"Yeah?" she said, intrigued.

"You should meet him," I said.

He's an interesting fellow. You two will get along well.

* * *

After I parted from Orga, I headed straight to the castle. I had planned to do laps like Rose had instructed, but I honestly didn't know where she'd wanted me to start. I ran along the castle wall, trying to figure out where to go, when I finally arrived at the entrance.

The castle was larger than I had remembered. I wasn't able to get a good look at it when Rose kidnapped me, but now that I was really seeing it I knew it was massive. As I admired the impressive door to the castle, I approached a guard who was standing nearby. The guard peered at me suspiciously until he saw my clothes, which somehow caused him to relax.

"Good day, Sir Usato, great member of the rescue team!!" he said.

"Um, hi," I said.

The man seemed very enthusiastic.

"What brings you to the castle today, good sir?!" he exclaimed.

"I'd like to go inside. Can I bring him with me?" I asked in the hopes he'd say yes.

"Is that a Blue Grizzly cub? Rose-sama has already received permission to bring him in, so it should not be a problem!" he exclaimed.

"What?! I can really bring a monster into the castle?!" I said in disbelief.

"Rose-sama has guaranteed our safety, so you can bring him on in!" he shouted.

Apparently, Rose had filled out paperwork that would allow Blurin to enter the castle. She probably thought I'd try to bring him, so she must have gotten it out of the way in advance. In any case, she was trusting me a whole lot. What kind of person was Rose exactly? I just didn't know anymore. I didn't know anything about her except that she was my captain.

"Okay, so I can bring him in?" I asked again.

"No problem at all, sir!" shouted the guard.

I carried Blurin on my back as I entered the door to the grounds that surrounded the castle. If Blurin attacked someone here, I would be the one to stop him.

"No misbehaving, okay?" I said.

"Grrr," he responded.

"Relaxed as usual, I see." Blurin was lying calmly on my back. If he stayed like this, I had nothing to worry about.

I didn't go inside the castle, but instead started jogging on the grounds in the hopes that I'd find the training area. Kazuki and Inukami had told me about it, so even though I'd never been there I knew what it would look like.

"They said it's a big open area, so . . ." I mumbled.

Even though I was the one searching, a part of me wanted to say, "what compass are you using to get there, dumbass?" Kazuki's descriptions were the only clues I had, so there wasn't much else I could do. Even so, I was sure that if I circled the castle, I would find it. I continued doing laps around the castle until I found a big open space.

"Whoa!" I exclaimed.

Dozens of knights were using wooden swords to train in the area. The invasion of the Demon Lord army's was imminent, so they were likely feeling quite shaken. While I was scanning the area, I saw a black-haired girl in the corner of the room. I was pretty sure I knew who it was. After I made sure it was her, I took a deep breath and called her name.

"Inukami-senpaiiii!"

*   *   *

I was in the middle of developing my final attack—an attack that was sure to cause a fatality. Magic training had already ended, so I decided to focus on honing my techniques. It was a final attack, so shooting lightning bolts just wouldn't do. It had to be different from my normal attacks. They say that men know more about these things than women, but Kazuki was clueless . . . or maybe he was simply indifferent.

"Inukami-senpaiii!" said a familiar voice.

I let out an audible "huh?"

When I turned around, I saw Usato running toward me.

However, I was totally frozen in place. How could I not be?! There was an actual blue bear having a good old time on his back!

"Usato-kun . . . What's with that bear on your back?" I asked.

"Oh! He's a monster called a Blue Grizzly, but he's still just a cub. He's pretty calm, so don't worry. He'd never attack," Usato said, placing the bear on the floor. He squatted down near the bear and started petting his head.

That's a monster. Why does Usato have a monster with him?

"Actually, I just came back from living in a forest for ten days! It was swarming with monsters. A lot of stuff happened, and before I knew it this little guy had decided to tag along," he explained.

"O-Oh. So that's why you haven't been at the rescue team

quarters lately," I said. But I was more curious as to why he was on castle grounds. "Did you come here to see me?"

"You and Kazuki visited me the other day, so I thought I'd swing by while I was training. Oh, wait. Is Kazuki not here today?" Usato asked, totally ignoring the fact that I was trying to tease him.

"He left the kingdom early this morning to gain experience fighting monsters. You just missed him," I answered.

"Aw, that's too bad. Why didn't you go with him, senpai?" Usato inquired.

"They can't have both heroes leave the kingdom, so I stayed behind. But don't worry about Kazuki-kun—Siglis is with him. Though Celia did seem a little down this morning when she'd heard that her hero was gone," I said.

Usato laughed. "Sorry to hear that, but I'm glad Siglis is there. Sounds like there's no need to worry," he said, breathing a sigh of relief. He was looking out for his friend, and that was great. More importantly, I couldn't stop thinking about the blue fluff in front of me.

"Grrr," the cub said.

"Hm? Sleepy already, Blurin? You haven't moved an inch, so I don't see how you could be tired," Usato said.

It was my first time seeing a wild bear, but it was a lot cuter than I'd expected. It reminded me of a panda I'd once seen as a kid. Whenever I thought of bears, I'd imagine ferocious beasts. But this bear was nothing like that. Instead, it was lying down and sleepily rubbing his eyes. It wasn't ferocious, it was downright adorable. In other words, there was only one question on my mind.

"Can I touch him, Usato-kun?!" I squealed.

"Hey! Don't say that so loudly! You scared me," he said.

"O-Oh. I'm sorry," I stammered.

I didn't realize how worked up I'd been. I guess I'd made a bit of a scene.

This isn't good. I gotta cool down.

"You can touch him," Usato said. "If he bites, I'll just heal you."

"Looks like I'm not the only one who says *scary* things," I quipped.

I tried to touch the bear's head, but he immediately slapped my hand down.

"Oh," I said.

I felt so . . . empty.

I'd waited so long for this moment only to be completely shut down.

I stared blankly at the hand that the bear slapped.

Usato spoke in an attempt to break the awkward silence. "Don't look so sad, senpai! H-He's just shy, is all."

"I'm not sad!" I shouted. "The touch of that little paw just got me excited!"

"You sound pretty confident, but I don't know . . . Why don't you try calling his name? He might let you pet him," Usato suggested.

"Okay, what's his name?" I asked.

"Blurin," he stated.

Blu . . . rin? That's one heck of a name. Usato's really got a talent for naming things, I see. I shouldn't have been so presumptuous. Of course, saying his name would let him know I'm a friend!

I reached out to touch him. "Oh, Blurin!" I said in the cheeriest voice I could muster.

But the bear sunk its teeth into my hand with a *homf*. It seemed like a love bite since there wasn't any blood. When he finally released my hand, it was covered in drool.

Is he trying to hide his embarrassment, Usato-kun? That's kind of exciting. But wait . . . animals should love me if I'm the heroine. For some reason, they don't. What does that mean?

"Looks like someone has a tainted heart," Usato said.

"Um, what? If that's the case, then why don't you try petting him yourself?" I replied.

"Just watch me," Usato countered. "Heh heh heh . . . Me and Blurin are buddies. Ain't that right, Blurin?" he said smugly.

The bear simply bit his hand with a *homf.*

I guess Usato had a tainted heart, too.

But despite being bitten, Usato was smiling. I was pretty sure he was bleeding—actually, I didn't care. Whatever it was, it was clearly a sign of Usato's affection.

Usato took his hand out of the cub's mouth, which prompted Blurin to look at me with a face that said, "Who, me? I didn't do anything wrong."

Umm. . . was Usato not hurt by that bite?

"By the way, what were you doing when we came in here, senpai?" Usato asked.

"Well, *that* was out of the blue. I was, uh. . ." I started.

"Were you training?" Usato asked.

What do I do? I can't tell him that I was thinking up a final attack! Usato is seriously training his butt off . . . he can't know that I'm worrying over something so trivial! He can't ever know. It's just too embarrassing!

"M-Magic practice," I lied.

"Oh, okay. Knowing you, I thought you'd be thinking of spells or a final attack," he said.

He must have read my mind. But in any case, this is a really good opportunity! For now, let's see if I can casually fish for info on some techniques.

When I asked him about it, he looked pretty suspicious, but he still answered me honestly. After we talked for about ten minutes, Usato suddenly seemed to remember something. He quickly got up and walked over to Blurin.

"Well, I should really get going," he said.

"What? Leaving already?" I asked.

"I've gotta get training, but I'll come back again soon. C'mon, Blurin. There's no time to sleep. Upsy-daisy. Ugh, I swear," Usato muttered.

He picked up Blurin and threw him onto his back. Blurin may have only been a cub, but the fact that Usato could carry him was—if anything—proof of how much he'd grown. When Usato left, I must admit . . . I missed him a little. Next time, I was going to visit him myself.

"I'm gonna do my best, Usato-kun," I murmured.

"Great!" exclaimed Usato. "And good luck coming up with a final attack!"

"What the?!" I stammered.

"See you later!" he said.

Before I could even say it back, he sped away from the training area.

How did he know I was thinking of a final attack?! Well, I asked him about it a bunch of times . . . maybe that's why he noticed.

"Okay. Time to get to work," I said.

I wonder if Usato realizes that he's being more open with me over time. Well, whatever. I'm sure it'll be fine.

CHAPTER 5

Usato Goes Back to the Forest!

A few days had passed since I'd visited Inukami. I was sound asleep in my bed . . . until I was rudely awakened before morning training.

"Hey. Rise and shine," someone said. I jolted awake.

Actually, I wasn't just rudely awakened—I had been *literally* drop kicked out of bed. Groaning as I fell to the floor, I glanced at the intruder who had disturbed my peaceful slumber. Unsurprisingly, it was Rose, who crossed her arms and looked down at me in an irritated manner. She was so intimidating that it would make anyone cower in fear.

"W-What's going on? It's still dark out," I said.

"I'll explain later. Get dressed," she ordered, then quickly left the room like the hurricane of a woman she was. Still half asleep, I changed into my training uniform as she had commanded.

"Okay. Gotta leave quickly," I whispered.

Now that I was fully dressed, I left my room and hurried to exit the quarters. When Rose saw me, she threw a square-shaped object in my direction.

"Take this," she said.

What is this, a backpack? It looks smaller than the one before.

Wait. Why am I feeling so shaky? Maybe I'm getting myself worked up for nothing.

"Huh? What's going on?" I asked.

"Just got a request from His Majesty. You're gonna join the heroes for training," she stated. I couldn't believe what I was hearing.

"Why the long face?" she probed.

"No, it's just . . . by heroes, do you mean Kazuki and Inukami-senpai?" I asked.

"Hero Kazuki's done training outside the country. Looks like you just missed him. You gotta accompany Hero Suzune instead," she stated.

I'm gonna train with senpai outside the country?! But . . . why me? Siglis's men were there for Kazuki's training, weren't they? Why can't they handle this, too?

As if she knew what I'd been thinking, Rose heaved a sigh and put her hand to her head. "When you returned from the forest His Majesty asked that you join Hero Kazuki in his training, but I told him you couldn't. You had just fought that heaping pile of junk, so I figured you were too mentally drained to go back so soon. Now that Hero Kazuki has returned, His Majesty wants you to join Hero Suzune. Naturally, I rejected this request too, but he keeps pushing and I can't keep turning him down."

She knew that I was exhausted after I came back from the forest. That was nice of her to notice. I'll give her that.

"But . . . why me?" I wondered.

"You can heal her if she needs it, but usually it ain't necessary," she said.

It almost sounded like she okayed the request because she knew I was far away from my friends. In other words, she entrusted me with my very first mission! Plus, my mission was to accompany Inukami, which was all the more reason to shoot my best shot.

"Right. Let's head to the gate," she said.

"Understood. Oh, what about Blurin?" I asked.

"He can tag along," she stated.

"Okay!" I said excitedly. "I'll go wake him up,"

I quickly went to the stable to find Blurin. It was the perfect opportunity to bring him to the outdoors. The open space that surrounded the training grounds was a decent size, but it wasn't the same spacious forest that Blurin used to call home.

When I arrived at the stable, I found Blurin curled up in a ball. He was sleeping on a pile of hay.

"Wake up, Blurin," I said, shaking him gently.

Blurin responded by groaning in his sleep.

"Urgh. You're out like a light . . . the captain's gonna kill me if we're late. Come on. Get up and start walking," I urged.

I spun the backpack to the front side of my body, then hauled Blurin onto my back. He was sleeping like a baby on the guy who was literally just kicked awake. What did he think my back was? A business class seat or something?

As I grumbled about Blurin under my breath, Rose rolled her eyes as we traveled to the the door leading out of the kingdom.

Dawn had barely broken in the empty castle town when we arrived at the door to the outside world. We spotted two guards who were standing close to Inukami.

"What are you doing here, Usato-kun? Did you come to see me off?" Inukami asked.

"Good morning, Sir Usato!" said one of the guards.

"He's here," said the other.

Two guards were there to protect Inukami: One was the overly energetic gatekeeper I'd seen at the castle the other day; the other was an unfamiliar woman who was wearing a black robe. The energetic gatekeeper removed the helmet that he had been wearing to reveal his short, red hair and nice-looking face. The black-robed woman, on the other hand, kept to herself. Judging from the shape of her body, I assumed she was a mage who worked for the kingdom like Welcie.

"No way. The last person to join us is . . ." started Inukami.

". . . probably me," I answered.

By "last" she must have meant that I was the final member in this four-person party.

Rose glanced at each of the members, then she scowled at the gatekeeper—who I believe was named Thomas—until he fearfully opened the door. I was so busy feeling sorry for him that I almost didn't notice that Rose had approached Inukami.

"Hero Suzune. Usato's healing magic should help you push past your limits. He's ready for battle, but just to be safe, don't assume he'll be able to pick up the slack," she said.

"N-Noted. This is my training, after all, so I will avoid relying on him as much as I can," Inukami answered. She seemed a bit overwhelmed.

"It's too early to know that for sure. Healing magic's useful but it ain't perfect. We can heal poison and wounds, but if you die, you're done for. I'll say that again: Don't rely too much on healing magic. Got it?" Rose warned.

"Y-Yes. Understood," Inukami answered, her voice slightly wavering. She stood frozen in place.

It sounded like Rose was telling her not to go overboard. From my perspective, Inukami wasn't prepared for the danger that lay ahead. This was probably because she was really enjoying this world and hadn't experienced actual danger.

"Well, you've been training under Siglis," Rose said, "so you should be okay for the most part."

After that, Rose walked up to me. She looked at me for a few seconds without saying a word. Despite shifting nervously, she patted me on the back, which signaled that she wanted me to walk to the door.

"You know what you have to do. Now get going," she said.

"That's it?" I inquired.

"What? You *want* me to talk?" she asked.

Actually, no. No, I didn't. Even if she gave me a pep talk, she'd end up criticizing me and that was the last thing I needed. Rose saw me slump my shoulders in defeat and she cackled as she walked away. When Rose was out of sight, Inukami let out a huge sigh of relief.

"No one has ever made me so nervous," she muttered, her voice still shaky.

"And that's her at her nicest," I said with a grin. "Usually, the captain never gives us any advice."

Inukami's face was still pale. "Your teacher's so hard-core," she said.

I wasn't sure what she'd meant, but even if I'd asked her, I knew she wouldn't tell me. Feeling a little uncertain, I set out with my party as we left the kingdom.

*   *   *

"How did Kazuki handle his training?" I asked.

"I heard he did really well," Inukami responded. "We're not used to fighting in actual battles, so he was understandably exhausted. He's been sleeping since yesterday."

"I hope he's all right," I said.

We made casual conversation as our party walked on a dirt

path outside of the kingdom. It was the same path I had taken when I came here with Rose. There were apparently few monsters around, so enemy encounters weren't likely unless there was an emergency. In fact, I wasn't attacked the last time I'd walked this path either.

The two guards were a few paces ahead of us. They remained incredibly focused as they watched out for potential attacks, proving that they could be trusted to guard Inukami. My only talent was using unskilled physical attacks, so I was sure they could easily beat me in battle.

"Is Blurin going to sleep the whole time?" Inukami asked.

I wasn't sure what she was getting at. "Pardon?"

"Oh, I was just wondering when you think he'll wake up. If he's sleeping . . . maybe he won't mind if I pet him," she said.

Is that all you ever think about, senpai?!

On top of that, she was basically hyperventilating as her fingers wriggled in the air above his head. I stared at her coldly as she approached him. She wanted to touch him a little *too* much. I was hoping she'd be as calm as when we'd left the kingdom, but that didn't seem like it was going to happen.

"He's sleeping, but . . ." I started. But the moment I opened my mouth, Inukami's arms moved so quickly that I'd thought we were being attacked. I ended up slapping her hand with my right hand out of reflex. Inukami brought her hand to her chest and looked at me in disbelief. A few seconds later, she suddenly yelled, "Why?!"

"I should be asking *you* the same thing! That was too sudden! Otherwise, I wouldn't have accidentally slapped you!" I responded.

"That's how you act when you slap a maiden's hand? Well . . . just look who's awake," she growled, angrily staring at me.

I didn't know what she was talking about, so I ignored her death stare. Seconds later, I realized that Blurin had finally woken up and was opening his mouth wide to yawn. I asked the two guards to stop walking for a moment while I placed Blurin on the ground.

"Go on. You can walk," I said.

"Grrr," he replied.

Blurin slowly stood up on his four legs, waddling side to side as he walked. Watching him, I sighed without thinking. I was hoping that he'd start walking normally if I just left him to it. I told the guards that they had nothing to fear, so the two of them kept walking.

However . . .

"H-Hey, Blurin . . . let me give you a piggy-back ride! Let's go!" exclaimed Inukami.

Wait, wait, wait, this is gonna be a disaster! He's still half-asleep so he might mistake you for a—oh.

The next thing I knew, Blurin was basically sitting on top of Inukami. To say she was having trouble holding him up would have been an understatement.

"S-Senpai?!" I exclaimed.

Did the prettiest girl in school just grunt like a man? I'll pretend I didn't hear that. Anyway, I've gotta do something before Blurin kills her!

I removed Blurin and rescued Inukami as fast as I could.

"Ack. I'm sorry, Usato-kun. I saw an opportunity and I went for it," she explained.

"I don't know what opportunity you're talking about, but please try not to get hurt. We're supposed to get injured during battle, not before it," I scolded.

She was tougher than I'd expected, but there was still a chance that her bones or internal organs were hurt. I enveloped her body in first aid magic as I continued walking the path.

"Are you all right, Madam Suzune?" one guard asked.

"I've got Usato, so I'm feeling just fine," she remarked. "Wow, you're amazing. My body feels so much lighter!" she exclaimed.

"Right . . ." I said, thinking about how her statement sounded kind of dirty.

I had placed my hand on Inukami's shoulder, but it was only because I was healing her. I wouldn't even dream of having ulterior motives. If anything, I was taken aback by her words. Maybe fantasy worlds really did change people after all.

Now that Inukami was healed, I took my hand off her shoulder.

Speaking of which, I never asked where we're going.

"Excuse me," I said.

"Yes? What is it?" replied the red-haired gatekeeper in front of me.

"Can you tell me where we're going?" I asked.

"We will be staying in the grasslands, which is home to various monsters. It is quite close to a forest that is called the Den of the Beasts, so there should be many fiends prowling about!" he exclaimed.

In other words, we were going to see monsters that lived in the same forest Rose had thrown me into the other day. Last time, I didn't see too many monsters, but that was because I always ran away or avoided them.

"How long will it take to get there?" I inquired.

"I would say . . . we should be there by noon," answered the red-haired man.

We were going a lot slower than I had with Rose. The four of us were moving together as a unit, so it was only natural that it would take us more time. It had only been a few days since I had left the forest, but seeing it again made me feel a little nostalgic. Blurin must have felt the same way.

"Grrr?"

Or maybe he didn't. After all, he left the forest so that we could travel together.

My eyes were fixed on Blurin when Inukami suddenly tapped me on the shoulder. "Actually, I was hoping you'd let me touch Blurin," she said.

"Haven't you already learned your lesson?" I asked.

She's a persistent one, I'll give her that. But if he crushes her again, I ain't helping.

A few hours had passed since we left the kingdom. Upon approaching the outskirts of the forest, the two guards halted in place.

"I'm sensing much movement ahead," said the mage.

"Is it monsters?!" Inukami exclaimed.

As the gatekeeper reached for his sword, we were ambushed by something that hid in a cloud of dust. When I saw its true form, I was at a total loss for words.

"Bandits! You two, stay back!" the mage ordered.

"Usato-kun . . ." murmured Inukami.

I could only say, "What the hell's going on?"

I never would have guessed that Inukami's first real fight was going to be not with monsters, but with people! There were fifteen bandits who wielded Western-style knives and swords that were chipped. They were blocking our path about ten meters ahead.

The gatekeeper wielded his sword as the mage held out her hands. As nervous as she was, Inukami also reached for the sword. For some reason, seeing the flippant grins on the bandits' faces made me feel calm.

A stout, bald man started laughing. He seemed to be their

leader. "Who'da thought we'd find treasure all the way here! It's our lucky day! Ain't that right, boys?" he called out.

"Yeah, boss!" his underlings answered in unison.

Ugh, this isn't scary at all. They lack a certain something, but I'm not sure what it is.

"Bwa ha ha ha! If ya don't wanna get hurt, hand over the goods!" the leader said.

"Never!" said the gatekeeper.

The bandits cackled crudely in response.

"Oh? You really think you can win against all of us? Don't make me laugh!" the leader sneered.

Inukami stood beside me and slowly tugged on my shirt.

She may be eccentric, but she's still a girl. Of course, she'd be intimidated by a bunch of guys cackling like hyenas. How could she not be? I should probably say something to her to calm her nerves . . .

"Can you believe it, Usato-kun?! Look! Real live bandits!" she exclaimed.

"You're really something else, senpai," I said.

I had forgotten that she was no average girl. I was the stupid one for forgetting that everything about this world was exciting for her.

After exchanging a few unkind words with the armed gatekeeper, the bald leader glanced over at me and Inukami. The man chortled as the corners of his mouth twisted into a grin.

"So the kids behind you brought their loot, too. Ain't no way you won't be handin' it over!"

"You will not be laying a hand on these two, you brute!" the gatekeeper said.

"Brute? Hah! We consider that a compliment! Wait—they have a monster!" said the bald man, who had spotted Blurin. A few seconds later, the color drained from his face. He started to panic. "Th-That's a Blue Grizzly! What the hell're you doing bringing that thing in here?!" he shouted.

"You're just a cub but you're really strong. Aren't you, Blurin?" I said.

Blurin snorted proudly as if to say, "Of course!"

It would have been more convincing if he actually trained for once, but I digress. My eyes shifted from Blurin to the bald leader, who was being consoled by his henchmen.

"Hey, Boss! That thing's just a kid! We can take 'em!" one said.

"Yeah!" shouted another.

"Boys . . . you're right! We clawed our way through them grasslands and ain't nothin' can scare us! C'mon, boys, let's get 'em!" shouted their leader.

He needed to be comforted by his henchmen?

This guy had no dignity. And from what they'd just said, I'd wager that their clothes and equipment were worn out because they had just crossed the grasslands. I didn't know how strong they were, but if they could make it through such a dangerous place, we couldn't let down our guard.

The bandits charged at us with their weapons as our guards got into fighting position. The truth was that I couldn't fight. I never learned martial arts or fought with a sword, and my training never involved one-on-one battles. I didn't know if I could fight like a real soldier should. However, I was an expert at running around the field to make sure that I didn't get captured. When it came to escaping, no one could do it better than me.

I readied my healing magic and leaped back as I focused all my strength to my legs.

But at that moment . . .

"Take this!"

A flash of lightning flew past our two guards and directly hit one of the bandits. The injured man shrieked as he convulsed on the ground. Unable to believe what we had seen, the bandits and I immediately looked at senpai's fingers, which she had pointed at them like a gun. The gatekeeper turned back to Inukami with a gallant smile on his face.

"That's Madam Suzune for you! Heh heh! She's so good that we don't even have to attack!" he said proudly.

Did she just zap him until he passed out?

"Y-You didn't kill him, right, senpai?" I stuttered.

"O-Of course not . . . I think," she answered.

Why did she hesitate?! Now I'm scared.

After witnessing Inukami's attack, the bandits stopped dead in their tracks. One of the henchmen ran to the man on the ground and nervously checked if he was alive.

Self-defense is good and all, but killing? If it's not too late, I can still heal him.

"H-He's alive," said the henchman.

Hearing this, Inukami heaved an audible sigh of relief. But this was a great diversion. At this rate, her lightning bolts could make quick work of the bandits.

"I'll heal you if I have to, senpai. For now, please attack all you like!" I said.

"You're the sweetest, Usato-kun," she said.

What are you saying?! I'm just trying to support you so you can feel free to strike down the bandits!

"D-Don't let her intimidate ya, boys!" yelled the leader. "Magic only works from far away! If we tackle her all at once, she's done for!"

"Go, Inukami-senpai! Mow 'em down!" I said.

"You don't have to be so crude, ya know!" she replied, then shot countless lightning bolts from the tip of her finger. Another man slumped to the ground, then another. She paralyzed the bandits and made them black out, which could only mean . . .

"You're a human stun gun!" I said. "No, wait, 'electric eel girl' is more like it!"

"You say that again and I'm gonna get angry," she threatened.

As the bald leader watched his henchmen fall face-first to the ground, he pointed at Inukami and bellowed, "You can't use magic! That's cheating!"

He was so lame that I just didn't get it. The only thing that was brutish about him was his face, but that's it. They weren't as vicious as Rose or the trainees, so this didn't scare me at all!

Inukami was about to round up the rest of the bandits when the mage suddenly spoke. "Something's coming. It's . . ." the mage trailed off.

It seemed that she had sensed something new. I couldn't see it, but I could clearly hear it approaching. The footsteps weren't normal. Whatever it was sounded like it was bouncing.

"Here it comes!" the mage shouted.

The bald man wore a dumbfounded expression.

"What's that?! Well, it's too late now to surrend—agh!" he screamed.

A red boar flew into him and sent him flying.

"Boss!!" his men yelled.

"Sir Usato, Madam Suzune! It's a pack of Fall Boars! Stay back!" the mage yelled.

"Why are they here? Their habitat is much deeper in the forest," the gatekeeper said.

The Fall Boars—red-haired monsters who had abnormally developed hind legs—had inserted themselves into the fight. The two guards swiftly evaded their attacks. However, three of them ambushed me and Inukami. As I locked eyes with one of the boars, I yelled Blurin's name so he could attack.

"GRAAAAAH!" Blurin roared.

Blurin stood up on his hind legs and ferociously spread out his arms, but the boars were too enraged to back down. Blurin managed to stop one of the boars in its tracks. The other two kept rushing toward me and Inukami.

I could take the hit. I knew I was strong. Inukami, on the other hand, likely needed assistance. I tried to fend them off to protect her . . . but she jumped right in front me and shot powerful lightning bolts from her hand before I even knew she was there.

"Get back, Usato-kun!" she yelled.

"Inukami-senpai?!" I shrieked.

Her lightning bolt struck one boar. The other had dodged it.

"Oh no," she said.

Fall Boars were unique in that they could jump incredibly high due to their unnaturally mighty hind legs. They were known to save up their power for a devastating attack; they would send their enemy flying high into the air and then slam them into the ground. Worst of all was the fact that Inukami was their target. Perhaps they had sensed that she was a bigger threat than I was.

I quickly grabbed Inukami's shoulders, switched places with her, and held on to her tight in an attempt to shield her. A few moments later, I had the wind knocked out of me from behind and was sent flying into the air with Inukami.

Luckily, my backpack took the brunt of the attack, but I

still grit my teeth as I tried to endure the pain that ran through my body. I felt like I was going to crumble at any second, so I quickly cast healing magic on myself to avoid blacking out. It was only then that I realized that Inukami had fainted in my arms!

"Senpai!!" I screamed.

I held her head tight as we fell to the ground and, while the leaves beneath us had softened our fall, we fell onto an unfortunately steep slope. We rolled all the way down the hill, going so fast that we were unable to stop. Every time the backpack hit the ground, it sprung us into the air only for us to be flung back to the ground twice as hard.

I screamed in terror as my vision went black; my entire body took a thrashing as we rolled down the hill and, eventually, were flung into a river. I tried swimming Inukami to shore, but the current was so strong that I couldn't fight it. I had no choice but to float down the river, but that was when I suddenly recognized the scenery around us.

When Rose had thrown me into this forest, I had jumped into this river to escape the Grand Grizzly. In other words, this river only led to one thing.

"Pretty sure there's a waterfall."

I wanted to take another path down the river, but the sound of the approaching waterfall made it clear that this was now the worst-case scenario. My only hope was to go over the waterfall, where the current was smoother. Then, I could likely bring her to shore.

"No choice but to brace myself," I said.

I held Inukami tight in my arms and took a deep breath.

*   *   *

". . . -kun! . . . Usato-kun . . . !"

I heard someone calling my name as I drifted back into consciousness.

I couldn't move a muscle. My arms and legs were as heavy as lead and my clothes were so wet that they stuck to my skin. I could only hear the sound of harsh, rushing water as a voice kept calling my name.

"Usato-kun . . . I'll take you somewhere safe! Just hold out until then!"

That was when I regained consciousness.

After we fell into the river, I used my last ounce of strength to carry Inukami to a nearby shore and passed out shortly after. Now that I was awake, the first thing I wanted to do was use healing magic to relieve my fatigue. I also wanted to escape Inukami's arm, which was wrapped around my shoulder.

"I will protect you. I, Suzune Inukami, vow to return this debt if it's the last thing I do!" she shouted.

"That won't be necessary, senpai. Actually, can you stop?

This is kind of embarrassing," I said.

"A-Awake so soon?" Inukami blurted out.

Now that my vision was no longer blurry, I saw Inukami clearly standing before me. She quickly stepped away from me and her face was bright red. She must have been embarrassed because I'd heard her impassioned declaration. If she wasn't embarrassed, then I didn't know why she was averting her gaze.

"Are you okay, senpai?" I asked.

"I-I should be asking you the same thing," she answered.

"I'm okay. This stuff doesn't faze me," I said.

As I surveyed my surroundings, I enveloped her in healing magic just in case she was hurt. I saw a familiar set of spooky trees and a waterfall, along with the sound of beastly cries in the distance. There was no doubt in my mind—this was the same forest that Rose had thrown me into. After making this grave discovery, I quickly told Inukami where we were. She understood what I'd said just as fast and then sadly hung her head.

"I'm sorry, Usato-kun," she lamented.

"No need to apologize. We're in this together," I said.

"Yeah . . ." she replied half-heartedly.

As much as I wanted to cheer her up, I was doing all I could to figure out how to get out of here. I had to do this, since I knew the terror of this place better than anyone else.

"Dangerous monsters lurk in this forest—ones that can even make quick work of the Fall Boars," I explained.

"We've got to get out of here quickly," she said.

"It's dangerous. Later in the day, there's only darkness. You can't see anything. No matter how strong you are, senpai, there's no way we can fight monsters that can ambush us at any second," I stated.

"True," she admitted.

The nights in the forest were always pitch-black. Traveling at night wasn't advisable, as the only thing that could guide us was the light of the moon.

"That's why we've gotta wait until daybreak to move," I said.

"But aren't we susceptible to attacks at night?" she inquired.

"I climbed a tree so monsters wouldn't notice me. Can you do that, senpai?" I asked.

"I've never climbed a tree before. My parents never allowed it . . ." she trailed off.

If she wasn't allowed to climb trees like the other kids, she must've been the daughter of a high-class family. I can totally see that being the case. Anyway, it sounds like tree-climbing is out of the question. In that case . . .

"Why don't we stay here?" I suggested. I pointed at the shoreline near the waterfall directly below me.

"Are you sure?!" she gasped.

"That way we'll always be close to water, at least. We can search for a better location, of course, but if we do that we'll probably just get attacked again."

"Y-You have a point," she stuttered.

"Then it's settled."

Inukami and I started gathering all the leaves and branches that had fallen to the ground. We managed to make a decent pile in a matter of minutes.

"Use your magic to set it ablaze, senpai. A fire might attract monsters, but at least it's better than being blinded at night," I suggested.

"I see. Understood."

She then zapped the branches and trees and set it ablaze. The fire burned brightly, expanding as it released smoke into the sky. I put my hand near the fire as it warmed up my body. Since I was in frigid wet clothes, I was thankful for the warmth.

"Do you have any supplies?" I asked.

"Yeah, in my backpack," she answered, taking out a small sword, a knife, and a map. The map wasn't useful, but the knife was sure to come in handy. I asked her if there was anything else in the backpack, but she only had a change of clothes and other personal belongings. She probably didn't think she'd have to survive in the wilderness, so I couldn't exactly blame her for not being prepared.

"I'm so glad my change of clothes didn't get wet," she said.

"Why don't you go ahead and change, senpai? I'll wait here. My clothes should dry up pretty quickly if I stay by the fire," I said.

"Yeah. But before I do that, take this just in case," she said.

She handed me the knife and the sword that was light enough to wield with one hand. Then, she took her clothes out of the backpack and carried them to a nearby bush. For some reason, she stopped in place and faced me. There was a devious smile on her face.

"No peeking, okay?" she said playfully.

The only word I managed to utter was, "What?"

"You don't have to shoot me down so hard, you know," she replied.

No matter where we went, I would never disrespect my senpai. After she changed, she acted like her normal, happy self. That made me relieved, but that's my little secret.

A few minutes later, Inukami changed into a simple outfit—a long-sleeved shirt and pants—and we started setting up camp. Honestly, it was a pretty simple setup; we kept the fire going and found somewhere to sleep.

In any case, the fire really was a game changer. It didn't exactly light up the forest, but we could at least see what we were doing at night. More importantly, having Inukami's magic meant that we didn't have to worry about food.

At that time, we were doing an experiment. Inukami's hand was in the water by the shore, next to a spot that was illuminated by the fire. "Does this work?" she asked.

"I'm ready to flee anytime, senpai!" I called out. "Zap it up when you're ready!"

"Zap it up? I wished you'd call it something else," she said, "but anyway, here I go!"

She zapped the water, which brought a few fish belly-up to the surface. Inukami wasn't happy that we were using her magic to catch fish, but I couldn't be happier with the results of our experiment. We had a new way to catch food and I was ecstatic. It was way better than the hard, stale rations I had to eat the last time I came to the forest. The only thing good about it was that it didn't expire, but now we had fish!

"I'm so glad you're here with me, senpai!" I exclaimed.

"Crying *and* praise? That's going a bit too far, don't you think?" she said, glaring at me as I thankfully bit into the fish.

It probably seemed like I was overexaggerating, but I didn't have to worry about fire or food, and we could even boil water to boot! With her by my side, this game of survival was simply too easy.

When we finished dinner, the sky was pitch-black. "It's pretty dark, so you should probably get to sleep. I'll watch the fire," I suggested. Inukami was sitting in front of me.

"No, I can't just leave all the surviving up to you. I'll watch the fire," she proposed.

"Let's take turns. I'll wake you up when I'm done, so you can sleep until then," I said.

I was too tired to watch the fire all night. We still had to survive, and the last thing we should do was push ourselves too hard in the forest. I could have used healing magic to reduce our fatigue, but magic power wasn't limitless and the day's events had really taken a toll on me. If we wanted to do well tomorrow, we both needed a good night's sleep.

"All right. I think I'll take a nap, then. No funny business," she said.

"I'd never," I replied. She seemed pretty shocked.

She sure picked a weird time to make jokes.

* * *

After Inukami had gotten some sleep, I managed to wake her up for her turn.

Ten minutes later, she suddenly asked me a question. "Are you awake, Usato-kun?"

"What's up?" I asked. I turned to Inukami to find her sitting on the ground with her arms around her knees. She was illuminated by the light of the fire.

"How did you feel when you were summoned to this world?" she inquired.

I didn't know what she was getting at. Maybe it was just a random question, or maybe something was on her mind. She could have even felt guilty that I was accidentally dragged into the hero summoning.

"How did I feel? Well, let me see . . . the captain's training was tough and every day I had to see the trainees' ugly faces. More importantly, we'll have to fight the Demon Lord's army. It still doesn't feel real," I said.

"Do you want to go home?" she asked.

"Hmm, I'm not sure," I answered.

I wanted to go home, but at the same time I didn't. There was a part of me that didn't want to let go of my new abilities—of the healing magic—that I had acquired. But more importantly, I didn't want to leave any of the people I had met in this world. I hadn't been here for long, but my experiences were greater than I'd ever imagined. But that didn't change the fact that I was worried about my family.

I was still trying to make up my mind when Inukami replied.

"As for me . . . I don't want to go home," she said, sounding nervous.

I didn't know if there was a deeper meaning to her words.

"Do you want me to ask why?" I asked.

"I do," she said.

She sure was blunt when she wanted to be.

I sighed. "I think I can imagine why you don't want to go home. You like this world better than Earth, plain and simple. Is that right?" I asked.

"Yeah," she replied.

Inukami was happier and more energetic after she came to this world. She was like a completely different person than the one I imagined her to be back home.

"I don't feel attached to Earth. My friends and family. . . they're just transient things that I've already abandoned. I plan to stay in this world. I've been waiting for a chance like this all my life . . . for a chance to finally be free," she explained.

The old Inukami was perfect—the girl who was out of everyone's league. But that perfection was nothing more than a mask that she had abandoned, or at least, that was how I understood it.

"I was overjoyed when I first came here—you two being here was a bonus. Nothing in this world ties me down. I wouldn't trade this freedom for anything," she stated.

I knew that she was happy, but I didn't know that she had decided to never go back.

"If you don't want to go home, sounds like staying here is for the best," I said.

She seemed confused. "What?"

"Why are you looking at me like that? Did you really think you were going to disappoint me if you stayed here or something?" I asked.

"Well, no . . . I just wouldn't be surprised if you were," she responded.

"I've always loved fantasy worlds. I just don't have as much baggage as you," I replied. I sat up and looked at Inukami, whose eyes almost seemed to be trembling.

"I've always wanted to change who I am . . . for the days of monotony to be turned on their head. I'm just like you, senpai," I said.

"Usato-kun . . ." she murmured. She sounded weak, which was very unlike her. The Suzune Inukami I knew was a more dignified girl.

"It's like I said back at the training grounds. I don't want to slow you and Kazuki down," I said.

"Right . . ." she replied.

"Back then, my plan was to just plow through my training. But I'm a member of the rescue team now. I've vowed to protect you and Kazuki, and even the people of this country. Do you have a mission, senpai?" I asked.

"I want to protect this country as a hero . . . no, just as myself. I want to protect the place I belong," she said.

"So you, me, and Kazuki . . . let's save the people of Llinger Kingdom together. Regardless of what happened on Earth, let's save the kingdom to protect the place we belong," I proposed.

Inukami and Kazuki would fight as heroes, and I would heal soldiers as a member of the rescue team. To me, that was ideal.

"You've gotten a lot stronger," she said.

"And you've become more open," I said. "I absolutely adored you back on Earth."

"Well, that's certainly honest. You can adore me more if you like," she quipped.

"You were a picture-perfect senpai back on Earth. You changed after you came here. You even said it yourself," I noted.

She laughed. "I can't deny that. But you know, I'd rather be close to you than be adored from afar," she murmured.

There seemed to be a lot of depth to her words.

She smiled calmly at me, but it made me feel a bit bashful.

I quickly lay down to escape from her gaze.

"It's bedtime. Good night," I said.

"Hm? Did I make you feel shy?" she asked.

I just as quickly turned my back to the fire.

If I spoke anymore, I'd be too embarrassed to sleep.

As I began to doze off, I heard Inukami giggle as she murmured one last thing.

"I'm really glad we got to talk. Good night, Usato-kun."

* * *

The next morning, Inukami and I started walking to try and escape the forest. I vaguely recalled which direction Rose and I took the last time I was here, so I was pretty confident that we were headed the right way.

"By the way, can Blurin track us by our scents?" Inukami asked.

"He could have . . . but then we fell into that river, unfortunately," I explained.

I just hope that glutton isn't eating the guards out of house and home.

We were walking slowly down the path. There were two reasons for this.

The first reason was to tread quietly. We wanted to avoid getting noticed by monsters at all costs. Kukuru wasn't with me this time, so there was no way to know if there were monsters around.

The second reason was to remember where we were going. Since the forest was filled with tall trees, rushing ahead would only make us totally lost. To avoid that, it was vital to take note as we moved through our surroundings. I'd learned this from the books that Rose had forced me to read.

Several hours had passed since we started walking the path, but there was still no exit in sight. Suddenly, Inukami spotted something flying through the trees above us.

"Usato-kun, up there!" she said.

I could tell something was wrong.

When I looked up, I saw a group of small monsters that looked just like monkeys. Their fur was a dangerous shade of green.

They must be . . .

"Venom monkeys," I said.

"You've seen them before?" Inukami asked in a panic.

"Only in books. This is the first time I'm seeing them in real life," I answered.

As one could guess by their name, the venom monkeys were poisonous. Though generally mild-mannered, they ate the fruits of poisonous trees to fend off their natural predators. When they consumed this fruit, their nails and fangs were filled with a potent venom that paralyzed their predators. This poison turned their fur green, which proved to be a powerful camouflage as well.

Just then, a young venom monkey strayed from the group and jumped in front of me and Inukami. I decided it was best to stand guard.

"That monkey's poisonous so you shouldn't touch it, senpai," I warned.

"Come here, li'l fella! Don't be afraiiid," she said to the monkey.

"Yo! Are you even listening to me?" I yelled.

There's just no helping her, is there?

I yelled at her gruffly because senpai was carelessly reaching out to the little monkey. She was honestly starting to give me a headache. The first thing I did was grab her arms, so she'd stop acting so crazy.

"You're gonna get hurt! That thing's poisonous!" I said.

"If it drowns me in poison, I must be fated to die at this cutie's poisonous hands!" she exclaimed.

She was trying to be cool, but it backfired.

"When will you stop saying such ridiculous things," I lamented.

I was at a loss. She was still a girl—at least by definition—so it wouldn't be right to grab her too hard. The little monkey stared quizzically at her outstretched hand, which only made Inukami smile smugly at what she interpreted as a friendly reaction. At least until . . .

"HOO!" the monkey screamed. It sunk its teeth into Inukami's pointer finger, but she didn't fret. Instead, she smiled stiffly as the monkey stayed glued to her finger.

"Come here, li'l fella. Don't be afraid," she said, this time a little more brusquely.

The monkey screamed once again.

After that, it ran away. Or maybe it would be more accurate to say that it returned to its group. I stood behind Inukami, watching as she sadly slumped over. I put my hand on her shoulder to heal the poison that had entered her body.

I tried to warn you, senpai.

"No reason to get all depressed, Inukami-senpai," I said.

But she didn't respond. I finished healing her and started walking away, but Inukami still wouldn't pick up her head. She seemed to be reeling from what had just happened.

Honestly, this is kind of annoying. I'm gonna ignore her.

Inukami started sulking. She wasn't pleased that I had stopped talking to her.

"Aren't you gonna comfort me?" she asked.

"I already did," I answered.

After a moment of silence, she said, "You're a meanie, Usato-kun."

Um, how am I the mean one in this situation?!

"I wish you would listen to me, senpai. What are you, an impulsive child or something?" I asked.

"Yes. I'm living my second life in this world, so in a way, I am a child," she remarked.

What kind of messed up logic is that?

I sighed in response, but Inukami didn't like that either.

"Why'd you just sigh like that?" she asked.

I decided not to answer.

"Ignoring me now, are you? Fine. Two can play at that game," she said.

Now all I had to do was keep ignoring her, since I knew that she would eventually talk. As we walked the path, I realized that the trees were thinning out with every step. It seemed that we were finally leaving the forest.

"We'll be out of here soon, senpai," I said as I turned back to Inukami, who was still keeping quiet.

"Tch. Of course, you'd speak when we're leaving. You have some sense of timing, I'll give you that much," she pouted.

But the only thing she was proving was that she couldn't hold a grudge. Even though she was making a scene, I managed to ignore her and keep my eyes straight ahead. A few steps later, we finally made it to a clearing that wasn't surrounded by trees.

"Sir Usato! Madam Suzune!" someone called out in the distance.

"That's the gatekeeper's voice," I said.

The gatekeeper had been searching for us all this time, and he was with Blurin!

"That was exhausting," I said.

But Inukami felt differently. "It's been fun. I liked being with you, Usato-kun."

Oh, brother.

Normally, I would think those words had meant something deeper, but this was senpai we were talking about. It was probably best to ignore it.

"W-We found you! What a relief!" the gatekeeper said.

Even Blurin growled happily when he saw me.

I started frantically waving at the two of them when Inukami suddenly turned to me and held out her hand. A cheerful smile—as bright as the sun—graced her face.

"We made it! Let's go home, Usato-kun!" she said.

I naturally smiled in turn, and while I felt a little bashful, I took her hand in mine. She was no longer the Suzune Inukami I had adored back at school, nor was she the graceful president of the school council. Instead, she was just a girl who enjoyed her new place in this fantasy world, even if she was brash and a little hyper at times.

"Yeah. Let's go home. Back to the place where we belong," I said.

Inukami nodded and smiled, which brought me great peace.

Maybe being more open with Inukami isn't such a bad thing after all.

*   *   *

Inukami and I safely made it back to the kingdom.

As it turns out, the gatekeeper felt responsible for us getting lost, so he and Blurin had spent the entire day searching for us without stopping for lunch. The other guard—the mage—had captured the group of bandits single-handedly. When she escorted them back to the kingdom she reported that we had gone missing. When I had the chance, I would definitely thank them both for their help.

Now that we had returned to the kingdom, we headed to the castle to tell the king that we'd made it back in one piece. The red-haired guard was babysitting Blurin; they had become fast friends, so I knew that they'd get along. He was nothing like a *certain someone* who kept trying to touch Blurin after he'd just slapped her hand.

Inukami and I entered the grand hall where the king had been waiting. Rose and Siglis were there too, along with a grumpy-looking old man named Sergio who had stood beside the king when we were first summoned.

The king saw us and immediately heaved a sigh of relief. "Oh, Usato, Suzune, I'm so glad you're safe," he said, slumping deeply into his throne. Judging by the bags under his eyes, it was safe to say that he had been worried sick. I opened my mouth to apologize, but Inukami beat me to the punch.

"We are sorry for worrying you, Your Majesty," she said.

"No need to apologize. We should be the ones asking you for forgiveness. We deeply regret all the hardship you've been through. I would also like to apologize to you, Usato. If I hadn't told you to accompany Suzune in her training, none of this would have happened," he lamented.

The king was so sensitive to the point where it was actually wearing him out. I was a little taken aback by his words. I knew I should say something in response.

"I-It's okay, really. It's kinda like, well . . . I'm already used to this sort of thing," I said.

"You are?" the king asked in disbelief.

I didn't know what to say. If I told him the truth, it would surely only make matters more complicated.

"Oh, uh, it's nothing! I spent a lot of time in the forest in my old world, so I'm just used to the scenery is all!" I lied.

"I-I see," he replied.

Why the hell did I just cover for Rose? Oh no, has she taken control of me to the point where she can control how I feel?!

I glanced at Rose, who was grinning, just as I thought she

would be. I had been utterly defeated. Just then, the king posed another question.

"By the way, how is your training with the rescue team? Has it been going well?"

There it is! The hardest question he could've possibly asked!

I had managed to change the subject a second ago, but then I was hit with another hard question! Rose was in the room, so I had to steel myself for what would happen later if I said the wrong thing.

"J-Just great," I stammered.

"Why, you don't say. I was worried about you, to be honest. But to hear it's going great makes me truly relieved," he said calmly.

My heart hurts so freaking much it's gonna explode!

I stood there, tortured by my guilty conscience, as Sergio turned to the king. "Your Majesty," he said, "it's almost time."

"Yes, I know," the king answered, then he turned back to us. "As for you, Usato and Suzune, I recommend that you take a rest. You must be fatigued."

After that, we left the grand hall just as the king said.

Rose was acting like her usual self, but for some reason Sergio and Siglis seemed very sullen. Just looking at their faces, I could tell they were relieved we were back, but something else seemed to be bothering them.

"Must be my imagination," I murmured.

I was fatigued and the king had totally called it. Inukami didn't look any more tired than she usually did, but deep down she must have been exhausted. We walked side-by-side for a few minutes, then prepared to head our separate ways. Right before I turned to say goodbye, I heard people shouting out of the blue.

"Usato! Senpai!" exclaimed a familiar voice.

"W-Wait up, Kazuki-sama!" exclaimed another.

A wheezing Kazuki and Celia-sama came running toward us. Kazuki put his hands on his legs and gasped for air.

"L-Long time no see," I said hesitantly.

"Don't *long time no see* me! I woke up and you and senpai were suddenly missing! Attacked by monsters, they said! I-I was so frickin' worried," Kazuki said.

Oh man, we must've really scared Kazuki. I feel bad for making him worry so much.

"I'm sorry," I said. And I really meant it.

The two girls were having their own private conversation when the princess suddenly looked at Kazuki and giggled. Every move she made simply oozed grace.

"When Kazuki heard that Suzune-sama was missing, he was so pale that I thought he was going to faint! In fact, he ran away from the castle to look for her," the princess stated.

"Ack! They don't need to know that," Kazuki said bashfully.

Inukami giggled. "Looks like you're just as reckless as us, Kazuki-kun," she jabbed.

"You're the queen of recklessness, senpai. You even got a little monkey to hate you!" I exclaimed.

Inukami grew flustered. "Urk. That's—you're such a meanie!"

"What little monkey, Usato?" asked Kazuki.

"Well, you see . . ." I started saying, but then she covered my mouth with her hands. Uhm, Inukami?!" I cried through her fingers.

"Ignore him! It's nothing!" she shouted. Maybe she didn't want the others to know. But in that case, I could just tell Kazuki later when we were alone.

Both Kazuki and the princess watched curiously as Inukami frantically pushed her hands to my face. The princess looked at me, then Inukami, then exchanged glances with Kazuki.

"They must be *really* close friends," she said slyly.

The princess seemed to have come to a grave misunderstanding, but Kazuki didn't quite know what she'd meant. In other words, I had to object before Inukami made the situation even worse. If I didn't clear the air now, the teasing would only balloon over time. To make matters worse, Inukami covered my mouth with a smile that was as curved as a crescent moon.

"No way. We're just friends. That would never happen," I stated.

Inukami suddenly backed away as if she were in shock.

I was hoping that she'd be less dramatic, but I guess that was too much to ask.

"Oh, really? Well, that's a pity," said Celia-sama, but her smile suggested that she didn't feel pity at all. It didn't matter what world this was—girls in any world will always gush over love stories. Not that this was a love story, of course!

"By the way, Usato, Rose-san is really incredible!" Kazuki remarked.

"Um, excuse me?!" I exclaimed. Rose and Kazuki weren't connected in any sense of the word, so hearing him mention her name totally caught me off guard. I trembled in fear as I waited for him to continue his thought.

"When I went to go look for you guys, Rose-san stopped me at the castle gates. She was the only thing that stood between me and the forest," he explained.

"She's a strange one, all right," I commented.

She treats me and Blurin like a baby, after all.

"I was being too hasty," Kazuki continued. "If Rose-san hadn't stopped me, I would've caused the country more trouble."

I couldn't deny it. If Inukami was missing and the only other hero was gone, the country would've flown into a panic. In that respect, Rose had surely done the right thing.

"What's more, Rose-san really believed in you, Usato," Kazuki said.

"She did?" I asked.

"She said you wouldn't die easily because you're her trainee. She never doubted that you'd come home safely. It was incredible how much she believed in you," he said.

Okay. So basically, she didn't think I'd croak on the spot.

Maybe I should've been happy that she trusted me, but I just felt conflicted.

Either way, I was moved that Kazuki was so kind and pure that he took Rose's words to heart. I looked at him sullenly and put my hands on his shoulders. He looked a bit bewildered, but I said what I felt I needed to say.

"Never lose that innocence, Kazuki. Don't become tainted like me and senpai," I said.

"O-Okay. Um, I don't really get it, but sure," he nodded, looking confused. Feeling incredibly reassured, I took my hands off his shoulders.

I let out a sigh of relief. . . but then noticed that Inukami was glaring at me.

I wasn't sure why.

"You just implied that I'm tainted," she said, looking incredibly unamused.

She's not denying it, so I'd say yes. Yes, she is.

*   *   *

After Usato and Suzune left the grand hall, Rose, Siglis, and Sergio stayed with me in the throne room.

"Do you know anything about the Fall Boars that attacked them, Sergio?" I asked.

"Not yet. I don't know what got into them," he answered sullenly.

Fall Boars lived on in the grasslands, but Usato's group had been attacked *somewhere else*. If this was nothing more than a coincidence, Rose and Siglis—the rescue team captain and the army commander—would have never been summoned.

"We interrogated the bandits that attacked the heroes beyond the grasslands. They said that there were fewer monsters than usual, but these people encroached upon our land from other countries. They are far from reliable," Sergio stated.

I put my hand to my head in dismay. "If the bandits are telling the truth, the monsters must have fled from their habitat in the grasslands. Something could have chased them into our country," I responded.

The enemy had arrived. War was forthcoming. It was safe to assume that they weren't going to underestimate us like they did in the last battle. Instead, they would launch an all-out attack to seize Llinger Kingdom.

Sergio broke the silence with a whisper. "It must be . . . the Demon Lord's army."

"Indeed," I said. "They have returned."

They were invaders whose demons and sinister monsters led the charge on Llinger Kingdom. I wanted to avoid all battles, if possible, but it was practically inevitable after the previous invasion.

"Siglis, tell the commanders to ready their armies. Prepare to attack," I ordered.

"Yes, Your Majesty! As you wish!" he answered.

"Good," I replied.

With a bow, Siglis exited the grand hall to go ready the army. Next, I glanced over at the woman who was crossing her arms and leaning back against a wall.

"Rose," I uttered.

"I know, Your Majesty. You want me to check how the Demon Army's invasion is going, don't you?" she assumed.

"My apologies," I said.

"Don't worry about it," she replied. "I know I'm the fastest person in the country. I'll go search deep into the grasslands, near the border. That sound about right?"

"Yes, I believe that is where they should be . . . though I'd much rather they not be there at all," I lamented.

There was a road in the grasslands that separated three different countries. The first country was Llinger Kingdom, the second was a neighboring country, and the third was the Demon Lord's Territory, a land teeming with monsters. A great river ran through the country.

"Right. I'll leave at nightfall," she said.

"N-Nightfall?! That's dangerous, Madam Rose!" Sergio warned, trying to stop her.

If the Demon Lord's army was indeed on their way, then hordes of monsters were on their way to our country. However, Rose would kick them out. She used to command an infantry division for the kingdom. She could make any monster turn on their heels.

Despite Sergio's warning, Rose started walking away.

I blurted out, "Rose, won't you lead troops into battle for us again?"

I knew she would refuse, but I couldn't help making a plea.

"I don't plan on returning, Your Majesty. I'm not as good as you think," she said.

"You were the first healer to be entrusted to lead the infantry division, so why do you criticize yourself so harshly? Even after you stepped down from your role, you have saved many lives as captain of the rescue team, have you not?" I asked.

"I'm not being critical. Just speaking the truth," she replied.

She possessed healing magic that gave her incredible physical abilities, which allowed her to destroy any powerful monster in her path. Her military service was so impressive that the knights still shared stories of her accomplishments, and she was even responsible for improving the reputation of the healers. As much as I wished she would step up to the throne as the Lieutenant Colonel . . .

"It's still bothering you, isn't it?" I asked.

"It is. I can't bring myself to forget. I accept my trainees' deaths. I know I can't bring my boys back to life, but this scar on my right eye just won't let me forget it," she said.

When Rose had risen to the rank of Lieutenant Colonel, she had trained seven of our most elite troops. They were spirited individuals who weren't easy to train, but all of them respected her as their commander. When her team set out to battle, they always secured an overwhelming victory, no matter how strong the monster or how evil the demon. With numerous achievements under their belts, no one imagined that their unit would suffer their ill-fated defeat.

"It wasn't your fault," I said.

"Yes, it was. My sense of pride led them all to their deaths. That's when I learned that no matter how much you train, no matter how incredibly talented and trustworthy you are, once you die, it's over. This scar is punishment for my sins. It won't let me forget what I've done," she said.

Her scar meant more to her than I knew. It reminded her of the death of the seven trainees she'd been entrusted with.

"Your Majesty, don't throw a gal into a battlefield who can't let go of the dead. I'm a good example of why you shouldn't," she reasoned.

She appeared to see the scar on her right eye as a symbol of proof for refusing to return to the army. But it wasn't just an excuse. What had happened must have traumatized her.

"That's why I made the rescue team. We don't fight; we're just a group that tries to save people's lives," she explained.

She had made the rescue team before the Demon Lord's resurrection. Many raised concerns about this incredibly odd organization, but public opinion swiftly changed during the invasion that took place two years ago, after the Demon Lord had newly risen. Rose and her elite troops saved many knights at that time, which ultimately led to our victory.

"There's one more reason why I made the rescue team," she said.

"What is it?" I asked.

She stared at me with the one eye she had left. I nearly shuddered when I found myself getting lost in her jade green eye, but I quickly readjusted my gaze to see her as one of our nation's leaders. The rescue team had contributed to our previous victory. Originally, I allowed her to create it, but she had never told me its purpose. I had a feeling that saving soldiers' lives wasn't the biggest reason she'd made it.

"I . . ." she trailed off.

She covered her right eye with her right hand. Her shoulders suddenly started trembling and her mouth curled into a smile. It was a face she normally never made, and with it, came words I never thought I'd hear her say.

"I want a trainee who won't die on me," she said.

A trainee who will never die. That was her wish.

While I recognized that it wasn't realistic, an image of a certain boy floated to my mind. It was the unlucky boy who got accidentally dragged into the hero summoning. At a glance, the boy was nothing more than an average, kindhearted, and perhaps unreliable lad. But now this boy had a duty to save the knights of this country.

Neither hero nor knight could master the exceptionally powerful offensive magic that Rose sought, and the boy was no different. Considering Rose's past, I could see why Rose saw so much promise in him. But expecting him not to die was just too much to ask.

"You can't expect people to live forever," I said.

"That's why we train. I seek healing magic, drills that allow us to do the impossible, and an iron will that won't bend to our enemies. I've been looking for someone who has all those things for so long and it looks like I've finally found him," she answered.

The one who had everything that she needed was . . .

"Usato, correct?" I asked.

"He couldn't be more ideal. He's just a kid who's only talent is healing magic, but it's perfect for the healer I need. Plus, he got used to life at the quarters much faster than I expected. Do you know what that means?" she asked.

"Do tell," I said curiously.

"He has survival instincts, adapts to his surroundings, and

has the will to live. If I'm being nice about it, this basically means he hates losing more than anything. The downside is that his environment basically shapes who he is," she explained.

"What do you mean?" I inquired.

"When the training's so tough that he's vomiting blood, he complains but he'll never stop going. I can scold him all day, but he never breaks down. It honestly feels like he was made for this world—to be a member of the rescue team. His personality meshes with everyone else's. He completed the rescue team's grueling training and survived for ten days in the Darkness of Llinger, and it's all because he did all he could to adapt to his surroundings," she said.

The will to live must have been in his blood.

"He's everything I need in a healer. And ya know, he fights me even though I put him through hell. Never bends to my will. It's almost as if he . . ." she trailed off.

She stopped her sentence short, shook off whatever thought she was having, and frowned once again. A few moments later, she looked up at me with a self-deprecating smile. As we stood in silence, Rose started to form a disjointed sentence.

"Yeah. He's just like a member of my dead crew. That damn cheeky brat. That's why I'll make him the best healer that ever lived," she said. Soon after, her heels clicked on the floor as she walked toward the exit. I was left alone, frozen in place.

It was the first time I'd seen her look so weak and forlorn. As I silently stood in the grand hall, I listened to the soft echo of her footsteps as they trailed off in the distance.

CHAPTER 6

A Night of Decisions!

In the Demon Lord's domain, near the country's border in the grasslands, a horde of demonic soldiers were building a bridge over the river that ran through the land. The soldiers were members of the Demon Lord's army who had traveled far and wide to invade Llinger Kingdom. Their leader was Amila Vergrett, the third demon army commander.

"The bridge is almost complete!" she shouted, seemingly trying to get into the mood for the forthcoming war. "We are the Demon Lord's arms! We will fight until we crumble to dust, and even then, we will offer our strength to our Lord!"

The soldiers buzzed with excitement. Amila nodded, satisfied by the army's response, but beside her was a knight clad in black armor who let out a long sigh.

"Calm yourself, Commander. Honestly, you're being obnoxious," the man said.

"Well, excuse me," she retorted. "This is huge for us. Of course, I'd be thrilled. And how dare you say your superior is obnoxious?!"

"Oooops. My bad. I'm still getting used to it," the subordinate grumbled indifferently.

Amila was so furious that her veins were basically popping out of her head. "Why you . . . never mind. It doesn't matter how things were before. You are officially my subordinate. You *will* obey my orders."

"Riiight," the knight said apathetically. After that, he turned on his heels and walked away. Amila was left there standing alone with her hand to her head.

"Talented, but nearly impossible to control," she muttered.

"He's giving you a tough time, isn't he?" a voice said. It was Hyriluk, a fellow demon. He walked toward her with a flippant smile on his face.

"Oh, Hyriluk. What are you doing here? Shouldn't you be babysitting your *beloved* creation?" she asked.

She was referring to Baljinak, Demon-made Monster Prototype Seventy-Two, a tactical weapon he'd made for the war.

"No need to sound so sarcastic. Anyway, how is the bridge coming along? Construction going well?" he inquired.

"Should be done in a few hours," she murmured, glancing sidelong at the nearly finished bridge.

The bridge was composed of two things: half of it was timber from felled trees while the other half was a hodgepodge of materials they'd conjured with magic. The bridge wasn't quite sturdy enough to be considered "durable"—not even in jest—but it was still a crossable bridge, nonetheless.

"I'm just saying, if that bridge collapses, we're screwed. Not to mention how demoralizing that'd be for the soldiers," Hyriluk added.

"That's why we're monitoring the other side of the shore at all times. Can't you say something a little less . . . ominous?" she said.

Hyriluk laughed. "Fine, I'm sor—"

"Commander!" one of the soldiers interrupted. He was clearly out of breath as he ran over to Amila. "An unknown object is flying straight at us!"

"What?!" Amila cried.

Moments later, a giant tree fell into the half-finished bridge. It pierced the bridge, which started cracking and soon crumbled to pieces.

"W-Why?! What just happened?! The bridge! It's . . ." she stammered.

It happened so suddenly that Amila and Hyriluk were frozen in shock. When Amila finally snapped back to reality, she spotted something incredibly far away on the other side of the river.

The only thing she could make out was a distinct shade of green hair.

"Rooooooooooose!" Amila screamed.

Her anger was directed toward none other than the fiend who was laughing on the other side of the river.

*   *   *

To my surprise, I was actually given time to rest.

Yesterday, Rose returned to the quarters from the castle much later than me, then she ended up heading somewhere at night. Basically, that meant that I had the next day off.

"Then why am I going to the castle town?" I asked myself.

I was holding a letter from Rose and an almost-too-clean drawing of a map. The problem was that I drew too much attention from the townspeople. I was wearing my uniform, but I wasn't even training and had left Blurin at the stable.

Why is he just walking around?" a civilian wondered aloud.

"Good question," said another.

It turns out that the rescue team didn't stroll through town like normal people. Maybe I should have been shocked, but I wasn't. My mind must have been poisoned . . . along with the townspeople's as well.

I casually ignored the whispers in town as I followed my map. My goal was supposedly on a giant main road, which Rose had said was relatively easy to find.

"That must be it," I noted.

I spotted a white, brick building that stuck out among the various shops. The map was clearly pointing to that building, but I didn't know if that meant that I should go in.

On my way to the building, I noticed a familiar set of ears and a tail. A fox beastkin girl was staring at me from about ten meters away. She definitely caught me off guard.

That gaze . . . it's almost like she's reading my mind. This isn't good. I should probably stay away from that girl.

I quickly approached the building, opened the door, and went inside. Upon successfully escaping the girl's gaze, I closed the door behind me and found myself in a room that was surprisingly tidy and reminiscent of the rescue team quarters. I called out to see if someone was there.

"Hellooooo?" I said.

"Comiiing!" replied an energetic voice from the back of the building.

A few moments later, a young girl hurried to greet me. She was a little shorter than me and had blond, semi-short hair. She looked as lively as her voice had suggested.

"Hellooo! What business do you have with the Fleur infirmary today?" she asked.

"Did you just say 'Fleur'? Um, Rose-san wanted me to give you this letter," I said.

"Omigosh! Really?!" the girl exclaimed.

If I remembered correctly, Fleur—the healer that wasn't me or Rose—was Orga's last name. It seemed that I'd arrived at his office. I took one more look around the room, then handed the girl Rose's letter.

"Thank you very much! And with whom am I speaking?" she squeaked.

"I'm Usato," I answered.

"Usato? My big bro told me about an Usato . . . Wait! You're the new trainee!" she said.

"R-Right," I replied.

She was incredibly energetic—the type of girl I could see myself being friends with on Earth. There was no doubt in my mind that she was Orga's younger sister.

"I'm Ururu Fleur! And um, I'm eighteen years old!" she exclaimed.

"O-Oh! I'm seventeen," I mentioned.

"You're one year younger than me!" she shouted.

Her comment was so random that I didn't know what to say. The interesting thing was that she and Orga both told me how old they were when we met.

Must be a quirk in their family.

"So, where's Orga-san?" I asked.

"In the back with a patient. Wanna come see?" she offered.

I had no idea what kind of healer Orga actually was. Rose was the only healer whose magic I'd seen, so this seemed like a good opportunity to observe.

"Only if you don't mind," I replied.

"Of course! Right this way!" she exclaimed.

I followed Ururu to a room in the back of the infirmary. She quietly cracked open the door. "Can't speak too loud," she said, "that wouldn't be good. My brother gets distracted pretty easily."

"Okay," I whispered.

Ururu and I peered into the room from the doorway. Being sneaky felt kind of wrong, but with Ururu there, I was (pretty) sure that it was okay. From the small opening, I saw Orga standing next to a young boy who was lying down on a bed, and a motherly figure who was holding his hand. The child seemed to be suffering from some type of illness.

"You see that boy? A few days ago, he got a weird infection that made him super sick. The symptoms were so bad that his mom brought him to our office," she explained.

"I see," I replied.

Green magic power gathered in the palms of Orga's hands.

"Whoa," I whispered. I couldn't help but be impressed. Orga's healing magic was a deep, dark green color that left behind a clear trail. His magic was much more potent than mine—I knew because I used the same magic as him.

Orga held his hands over the child's head and chest, which sent a wave of healing magic over his body. Orga's magic was incredibly smooth. It was way out of my league.

A few moments later, Orga lowered his hands.

"All better," he said. He had instantly healed the child, who quickly sat up in bed.

"He's right mama, I'm cured!" exclaimed the child. "I feel so much better!"

"Amazing," I whispered. The once bedridden child now

seemed to have all the energy in the world. The child's mother bowed profusely to Orga. No matter how flustered he looked, Orga was an expert healer, plain and simple. I could never reproduce carefully crafted magic like his.

After he walked the mother and child outside the building, Orga came back inside with a delighted smile on his face. "Hey, Usato-kun! Nice to see you."

"Same here," I said. "Oh, and sorry for barging in while you were busy."

"Not at all! I'm happy you paid us a visit. Did Ururu-chan do a good job of inviting you in?" Orga asked suspiciously.

"Of course I did. Duh! Oh, feel free to sit down, Usato-kun. We can stand around and talk, but nothing beats being comfy," Ururu said.

I sat down in a wooden chair. Orga and Ururu sat down across from me at a table.

"Thank you for bringing us a letter from the captain," Orga said.

"No problem. I'm glad that I came. I wanted to see this place for myself," I replied.

I really meant it when I said I was glad that I came. Having the chance to see Orga's healing magic had made my whole day.

Did Rose want to show me his magic? Is that why I'm here?

"So, tell me, Usato-kun! How's everyone on the rescue team doing?" Ururu asked.

"You mean Tong and the others? Same as usual, I guess," I answered, grinning wryly as I answered her random question.

"Yeah, I can see that. They're not the types to change quickly, if at all. That's the rescue team for ya!" she squeaked.

Orga, who was watching our conversation play out, suddenly asked a question of his own. "Next time, why don't you try working here, Usato-kun?"

All I could muster was a bewildered, "Huh?"

"He'll never say yes to that, big bro! How could he when he's so busy with Rose-san's training?" Ururu said.

Orga chuckled. "Heh, guess you're right."

But Orga's offer didn't sound all that bad. I could probably learn a lot just by observing his magic. On the other hand, I really was busy with training.

Maybe if I ask Rose, she'll let me study under him for one day.

I gave a truthful answer. "I would love that, but I'll have to ask the captain first."

"I await the good news," Orga said. "It's no easy task running this place by ourselves."

"C'mon, Orga! Quit making us sound so helpless!" Ururu said.

Orga laughed. "You're strict, but I can't say that you're wrong."

It was clear that they were incredibly close. As an only child, I must admit that I was a bit jealous. But then I thought to myself: If Orga couldn't keep up with Rose's training, was Ururu unable to keep up with it too? From what I'd gathered from the conversation, she was also a healer.

"Why did you quit Rose's training, Ururu-san?" I asked.

"Welllll, even if I'm not as weak as my brother, I'm much better at healing other people than anything else. But the real reason I gave up was because . . ." she trailed off as she pointed at her brother, who was grinning bashfully while scratching his head. "I was worried about him!" she lamented, acting as though Orga was a troublesome child.

"Heh, sorry sis," Orga chuckled meekly.

Anyone would think that she's the older sibling—not him.

After that, we engaged in silly banter, and before I knew it it was already past noon. They invited me to eat with them, but I turned them down because I didn't want to impose.

"See you around, Usato-kun!" Orga said.

"Come again soon!" Ururu exclaimed.

"Will do! Thanks for everything," I replied.

After they bid me farewell, I left the infirmary. I was so busy training that I'd forgotten to rest . . . and it turned out that resting wasn't so bad. It was incredibly peaceful. *Too* peaceful. I was worried that Rose would get mad because I wasn't training, but then I realized how ridiculous that sounded!

She'd never do that! R-Right?

*   *   *

After I left the infirmary, I aimlessly checked out the stalls that lined the streets.

"I should probably get something to eat. Oh, wait. I didn't bring any money," I mumbled.

I had no choice but to go back to the quarters. I turned around to do just that when someone grabbed my arm. It was none other than the beastkin fox girl I saw before I had entered the building.

The beastkin girl whispered quietly as she stared into my eyes.

"You're the only one who can see it. That means that you can alter the future."

I had no idea what she was talking about.

In an instant, all sights and sounds turned to darkness. I held my head in agony, stunned by the illusions that filled my view like a daydream.

A vast, endless field.
The knights of the Demon Lord's army.
Dark-skinned demihumans with weapons.
A figure adorned in jet-black armor.
Kazuki and Inukami sinking in an ocean of blood.

It was the worst sight I'd ever seen, and on top of that, it was incredibly real. When my vision returned to normal, I desperately tried not to vomit. The beastkin girl was also holding her head as it dripped with sweat, just like me. Our eyes met again, prompting her to mumble under her breath.

"You have received an incredible debt. It is your duty to repay it," she said.

Debt? What does she mean?

Everything became blurry, and just as I thought I was going to fall to the ground, the beastkin girl held out her hand. I took one look at her hand and was filled with so much fear that I . . .

. . . simply started to scream.

I brushed away her hand and ran as fast I could without looking back. I returned to the quarters and curled up in bed, where I tried my hardest to forget the alarmingly real sights that I saw in my head.

"What the hell was that?" I murmured.

Despite lying in bed for a while, I couldn't get the fox girl's illusions out of my head. What was she trying to tell me? Did I really have a debt to repay? What kind of debt was it? Rose had mentioned that some beastkin possess special abilities. Did that girl have the ability to show other people illusions?

"Was that . . . the future?" I wondered aloud.

It was far-fetched, but it wasn't impossible.

Why would she show that to me? Is that really the future? If that's the case, Kazuki and Inukami are going to . . .

"No!" I shouted.

I heaved a deep sigh and laid back down in bed. Nothing made sense and it was bugging the hell out of me. Why did I have to be so nervous about a debt that I was being forced to repay? I didn't have answers, so I thought it best to ask the fox directly.

"Yeah. For now, I'm gonna get a hold of that girl and see what's going on," I said.

Now that I'd made my decision, I knew what I had to do next.

I was going to be as fast as the wind.

"Where the hell is that loli fox?!" I yelled.

The fact that I was having pervy thoughts wasn't because I resented her. Or at least . . . that was what I chose to believe.

First, I ran back to the place where the girl grabbed my arm. I was making such an awful face that I probably looked like a depraved freak, but the townspeople didn't seem to notice. Wearing that training outfit basically gave me permission to act like a weirdo. But if I were wearing normal clothes, then they'd really do a double take.

"She's not here!" I shouted.

Since she wasn't where she was earlier, I'll go to the stall where I first saw her. If I can just ask a shopkeeper about her, I'm sure to find her.

"It's closed!" I shouted again.

The store was never open to begin with. Yet another failed attempt.

After that, it was time to check the alleyways!

"It's too big! I don't know where to go!" I shouted once more.

I felt like a total buffoon. No matter where I looked, the fox girl was nowhere to be found. I asked the civilians about her on the street, but none of them knew a thing. What made matters worse was that they refused to look me in the eyes. Oh well.

After searching most of the main road, I went to the last place I could think of.

"The door that leads outside the kingdom," I said.

But even then, I wasn't expecting to find her.

"I haven't seen any fox beastkin around here," said Thomas the gatekeeper.

"Yeah, I figured," I replied, downtrodden.

I knew it. If she were there, that would make life too easy.

With slumped shoulders, I slowly started heading back to the town.

"After all that, I didn't get any info," I mumbled.

I had run through the town at full speed and searched every place I could imagine, but even so, my efforts had amounted to nothing. Was it possible that she had predicted the future and was now trying not to get caught?

"Stupid stuff like that isn't possible," I mumbled.

"What isn't possible?" a voice asked from behind. Without looking, I knew that it was the voice of my fiendish captain, who was already back from wherever she'd been.

I shrieked with surprise, then slowly turned around to see Rose. She was covered in dust for some reason. I wasn't sure what to say, but I blurted out something anyway.

"Well, look at you. You're such a good captain that even dust can't stay away!" I said.

"Aww, how sweet. Now get over here so I can strangle you," she threatened.

She's gonna pop me like a balloon!

Rose grabbed my face in her iron grip and held me up in the air.

Wait! I'm really sorry. Please stop! My bladder isn't that strong!

I struggled to escape, only for her to sigh and quickly unhand my face.

"Gotta report something to the castle. You're comin' too," she said.

"Fine. I don't care anymore, so just do what you like," I said.

I had escaped her iron grip, but then she scooped me up in one arm. She was holding me captive like some sort of prisoner.

She did that so casually. What does she think I am? A stuffed animal?

"What were you doing out here anyway?" she asked.

"Oh, I was just looking for someone," I answered vaguely.

". . . the hell?" she responded.

"Why the long pause?" I asked. "Well, whatever. I was looking for a beastkin fox girl."

"Ohhh, *that* beastkin. The same one you said that weird comment about earlier. What's up with the girl?" she said.

"Do you know anything about her?" I asked.

"She came to the kingdom two years ago. I was surprised that a twelve-year-old beastkin made it all the way here . . . but that's all I know," she explained.

So, a twelve-year-old beastkin escaped slave traders and bandits and made it here by herself? If that were true, the fox girl really was a master at hiding. Finding her seemed like an impossible task.

"I mean this in the nicest way possible, but really, don't do it," Rose suggested.

"Suddenly acting all nice just confuses me more," I said.

Seeing her filled with compassion was just too rare a sight! My eyes . . . they burned!

Go back to your normal self! Rose isn't nice! Plus, I'm not a pervert!!

Rose continued to toy with my mind while she carried me to the castle.

*   *   *

Rose carried me all the way to the king, who sat in the grand hall. She seemed to like how easy I was to hold and showed no signs of putting me down.

"Rose? Why are you carrying Usato like that?" said the king with widened eyes.

"I come bearing news. I have confirmed that the Demon Lord's army has stationed their men near the border," she announced.

"I knew it! How close is the Demon Lord's army?" he asked.

Rose was covered in dust from head to toe. She'd probably investigated their whereabouts on her own. Despite hearing that the Demon Lord's army was making their advance on the kingdom, it somehow still didn't feel real.

"They were building a makeshift bridge to traverse the river, but I demolished it before it was finished. This should give us a few more days to prepare," Rose reported.

The king's face was frozen in fear. "Th-Thank goodness," he said.

That didn't sound like "investigating" to me, but either way, she had accomplished an incredible feat. My captain was in a league of her own.

"Tomorrow, I will tell the citizens about the enemy army's invasion. I thank you for your work today from the bottom of my heart, and apologize for putting your life at risk," he said humbly.

"Don't worry about it. Now if you'll excuse me . . ." she said as she walked out of the grand hall. She was still carrying me, so naturally I left the room too.

"Before the war begins, I've gotta warn you about a whole bunch of things," she said.

"Like what?" I asked.

"Oh, important stuff. I'll tell you when we get back to the quarters," she stated.

I couldn't help but wonder what she wanted to say.

"Captain?" I inquired gently.

"What?" she asked.

"Isn't it about time you put me down?" I mentioned.

". . . I forgot I was holdin' you," she answered.

It wasn't exactly what I'd wanted to hear.

After spending some time in my room, I went to the captain's quarters to go talk to Rose. Her room was on the second floor, all the way in the back. I'd never been there, but I always knew she was there when we weren't training. I knocked on the door.

"May I come in? It's Usato," I said.

"Enter," she commanded.

I went into the room, which was a lot cleaner and more organized than I'd expected. Various books lined the shelves and there was a stack of documents piled high on her desk.

Rose was sitting at that very desk, her elbows resting upon it and her hair seemingly wet. She must have taken a shower to get rid of the dust.

"Sit," she instructed.

I sat in a chair that was awkwardly placed in front of the desk. She was staring right at me, so I found it impossible to relax.

"Do you remember what role you play on the team?" she asked.

"Um, I go out on the front lines like you and heal the wounded," I answered.

"Here's the deal: At the start of battle, you and I do *not* go to the front lines. First, you, me, Orga, and Ururu—the four healers—will heal the wounded soldiers that Tong and the others bring to us," she explained.

"Why don't we start on the front lines?" I inquired.

"When the battle's just starting, there ain't no one to heal. There's too much action on the front lines and it'd only make us sitting ducks," she said.

"You've got a point," I admitted.

I hadn't thought that far ahead. No one is wounded at the start of a battle. Without people to heal, we'd just get in the way.

"I want you to know the most important thing about going to the front lines," she said.

"What would that be?" I asked.

"I need to hear this just as much as you do, but . . . don't heal the wrong people," she murmured.

"Do you mean that we shouldn't heal the enemy?" I mused.

Why is she saying something so obvious? Why would we heal our attackers?

"No, you idiot. Just don't be reckless when you heal," she said.

"How so?" I asked.

"For example, let's say that one of our men is slightly wounded but keeps fighting. What would happen if you got careless and rushed to heal him?"

I paused for a second. "I'd just get in the way."

"Exactly," she said. "The battlefield is swarming with enemies. You have to decide who needs to be healed, and you've gotta do it fast."

Now I get it. I can't distract our men when providing support.

The strange thing was that Rose seemed different than normal. For some reason, she was being less thorny than usual. She was acting this way before we went to the castle, but she was even gentler now.

What inspired such a change of heart? Is she lifting me up just so she can break me down later? Wait. What's that flying at my—

I yelped as a white object was flung at my face.

"That's the official rescue team uniform. Try it on," she ordered.

I sat there bewildered, studying the white coat I was holding that looked like a doctor's lab coat. The cloth was smooth and durable. It was as thick as a luxury animal hide. A single red flower—the symbol of the rescue team—had been stitched onto the right side of the coat. It was the same uniform that Rose wore all the time.

"I made this so that we stand out on the front lines. Not only is it sturdy, but it's also resistant to water and dirt. It's one helluva coat, and it's yours," she said.

"Th-Thank you so much," I stammered.

This is kind of amazing.

I put my arms through the sleeves and buttoned the front of the coat. It was surprisingly light, easy to move around in, and comfortable, even.

"Well, look at that. It suits you fine. I guess . . . all your training was worth it," Rose said.

She suddenly closed the distance between us without so much as making a sound. Rose put her hand on my face, but I stood totally still. The reason I didn't fight her wasn't because I was scared; I felt that I had a duty to push my feelings aside and face her.

"Just because we're healers don't mean we're immortal. If you die, it's game over. The one thing you must never do on the battlefield is throw your life away. Do you understand me, Usato?" she said.

"Yes, ma'am. Believe me, I don't wanna die either," I answered.

"How stupid can you be?" she retorted, then flicked my forehead *hard*.

I was so taken aback by the pain that I started to groan, but then she grabbed me by the collar and put her face just a few inches from mine. She held my cheeks in her hands and forced me to look in her eyes.

"Talk all you want, but I know men who've said the same shit and winded up dead. I know fools who have so many regrets that they wish they would die," she whispered.

"Captain . . ." I trailed off. I couldn't bring myself to look into her eyes. Her words were as sad as they were deep.

"Don't take your life for granted," she said. "The rescue team can't survive without you, goddamnit. If I see any self-sacrificing crap, I'll beat your ass before the enemy does."

Sacrificing myself wasn't something I'd do. But if Kazuki or Inukami were dying, like they were in that vision . . . I didn't know what I would do. Would I rescue them even if that meant certain death? Or would I be so afraid to die that I'd escape by myself? Neither situation was good.

"Then I'll save everyone, including myself," I stated.

"Think you can do that, punk?" she inquired.

"You're the one who told me to speak my ideals, Captain," I replied.

We stared into each other's eyes as we stood there in silence.

A few seconds later, Rose let me go as a smirk played on her face.

"Don't you forget what I just told you," she said.

I fixed the collar on my uniform, then answered, "Yes, Captain!"

Her training might have put me through hell, but in that moment I realized that it had taught me more than I'd ever expected. I was proud to be a member of Rose's rescue team . . . but I could never tell her because it was just too embarrassing.

Anyway, she's gonna hate this, but . . .

"Your training's probably gonna kill me before the enemy gets to me anyway," I said.

"Shut up," she snapped.

The next thing I knew, she headbutted me so hard that I was seeing stars. As I slipped out of consciousness from the sheer force, I saw Rose touching the scar over her eye . . . and for some reason she was smiling.

* * *

When I opened my eyes, I found myself in my bed.

"I knew it!" I said. "Rose is the worst!"

After that, I thought I heard someone yell. Tong was the only one in the room, snoring in the bed next to me, so I figured I was imaging things. The uniform Rose had given me was hanging on the wall.

Who brought me to my bed? Did Rose do that?

"Tch. Did she headbutt me because she was embarrassed? Wait a sec. Did I hear someone screaming just now?" I wondered.

"U-Usatooo!" someone yelled. The voice was coming from outside my window.

But I'm on the second floor. There's no way someone would be all the way up—

"Over heeere!" the person said.

"Kazukiii?!" I exclaimed. My voice slipped into falsetto.

I glanced outside to find Kazuki dangling from the window's handle. Despite not knowing why he was there, I put on my shoes and went out the window.

"Why are you going down?!" he exclaimed.

"Why were *you* coming up?!" I shouted back.

I wasn't going to bring Kazuki into the room. Tong was sleeping, for Pete's sake! Plus, I'd have to risk waking up Rose, and I didn't want that. If she knew I was awake at this hour, I'd get a punishment so severe that even a demon would beg for forgiveness.

After Kazuki climbed down the wall, we moved away from the building. The light of the moon was bright, which meant we could walk without too much trouble.

"Why are you here in the middle of the night? H-Hold up. I don't like guys like that, okay?!" I said, shielding my body.

Kazuki looked confused. "What are you talking about?"

"Sorry," I said. "My mind was in the gutter."

Kazuki was so innocent. *Too* innocent. He was the complete opposite of Inukami. Anyway, since he'd come all the way here, we went to the training grounds where we could talk. We sat on the ground as I listened to what he came here to say.

"The king just informed me that the war against the Demon Lord's army is about to begin," Kazuki said.

"Oh, right," I replied.

The king was quicker than I'd expected. I couldn't imagine Inukami's reaction, but I totally understood why Kazuki was anxious.

"Senpai was a little taken aback, but it didn't take her long to return to her normal, happy self. Me, on the other hand . . . I can't stop thinking about the war. Keeps me up at night, you know? And before I knew it, I ran all this way from the castle," Kazuki said.

I didn't know what to say.

"I . . . ran away, Usato. I just . . ." he trailed off. He turned to me as his face gleamed in the moonlight. He normally looked like a dashing young man, but now there was a hint of meekness in his eyes.

"Fighting scares me," he admitted.

How could it not? Before this, we we were just average high schoolers on Earth.

"I left the kingdom the other day and saw my first monster. I was really, really scared. I almost thought I was gonna fall to my knees," he said.

I kept listening.

"After I vanquished the monster that desperately struggled against my attacks, I realized that I was naive when it came to this world," he explained.

He was incredibly sensitive, whereas Inukami was not. Inukami had accepted this world as her own, but Kazuki was overthinking things to the point of distress.

"When the Demon Lord's army attacks, they *will* try to kill me. That scares me more than anything else. I'm nothing more than a coward, yet the kingdom treats me with kindness, supports me, and even believes in me. I feel like a failure," he lamented.

He suffered because he'd been branded a hero. People looked at him with envy and reverence simply because they heard the word "hero." Kazuki couldn't handle that burden.

"I'm going too, Kazuki," I said.

He turned to me with a confused look on his face.

"I'll save everyone who fights the Demon Lord's army," I stated.

Kazuki seemed conflicted. Should he prioritize his true

feelings, or the expectations of the people? He didn't know what to do, so he looked to me for an answer . . . but I held my tongue. I didn't want him to fight more than he had to. But saying that would have been irresponsible. In the end, Kazuki should be the one to decide his own fate.

"Aren't you scared?" he asked.

"Of course. More scared than you think. But I've already made my decision," I said.

"You've already decided? Are you sure? You might die! They dragged you into this mess *and* they're making you fight?! That's just messed up!" he exclaimed.

When we were first summoned, Inukami thought that I would hold a grudge after being dragged into this world. It sounded like Kazuki felt somewhat guilty about this as well. Honestly, they didn't need to worry about me so much.

"A lot's happened since I came here," I mentioned.

Kazuki listened intently.

"It's been rough, but I've met so many people who accepted me even though I was brought here by accident. I wouldn't be where I am now without them. They've done so much for me. I want to support them in any way that I can," I said.

That was why I would enter the battle as a member of the rescue team.

"You're included in that, of course," I said.

"Really?" said Kazuki, looking surprised.

"For sure. Whether you fight as a hero or not, that won't change the fact that we're friends," I stated.

Wait, I'm not the only one who thinks we're friends, right?

Feeling a little uncertain, I turned to Kazuki to find him staring down at the ground. His hands were trembling. He looked like he was trying to stifle his emotions. I watched him nervously when he suddenly looked up and slapped himself in the face.

"K-Kazuki?!" I exclaimed.

"I'm such a pansy!" he said, turning to me. He had hit his cheeks so hard that they were already puffy and red. When he noticed that I backed away from him, he smiled his usual wonderful smile.

"I've made up my mind. I will fight to protect you and senpai!" he announced.

"Whaaat?!" I replied.

"I don't know if I'll be able to fight as a hero, but I will certainly try. I want to save you, Usato . . . because you're my friend!" he exclaimed.

I said I'm gonna save him, so why is he gonna save me?!

"H-Hold up. I know I'm not one to talk, but are you sure that that's what you want to do?" I said.

"You're ready for battle, so I can't run away like a scaredy-cat now! I have to dive right in. I'll face my fears . . . along with everything else in this war!" he said.

"Are you sure?" I asked.

"When I remember that you and senpai will be there, it makes me feel so much better! I'll be okay, I swear!" he exclaimed.

"That's more like it," I said, smiling as I turned to Kazuki. "It's up to us. Let's protect this country and everyone in it!" I said.

"Yeah!" he replied.

We smiled at each other, then reality hit me like a brick.

I was speaking from the heart, but I didn't expect it to sound so cringey!

Feeling incredibly embarrassed, I started to turn away from Kazuki. He bashfully scratched his cheek.

"I'm really glad I met you, Usato. Thank you," he said.

"M-Me too," I answered.

Oh god, this is so freaking awkward!

I wasn't used to people saying this stuff straight to my face, so it felt kind of creepy. The fact that Kazuki could say these things without hesitation was a good thing. But being on the receiving end was just kind of uncomfortable.

This doesn't suit me at all! I'm supposed to be more stoic than this!

Kazuki chuckled. "I should head back to the castle. Sorry for waking you."

"N-No prob," I replied.

"Well, have a good night!" he said. And with that, he took off.

He started jogging to the castle, guided by the light of the moon.

Kazuki looked fearless as he ran into the distance.

I watched Kazuki disappear into the night, then yawned loudly as I headed back to the quarters.

"Gonna head right to sleep. Yeah, sounds like a plan," I murmured.

I was hoping that a good night's sleep would help me forget all the cringey stuff.

"Well, well," a voice chimed in from behind me, "I guess that's what friendship between guys is really like. Almost brought a tear to my eye."

I knew who it was, so I didn't bother turning around.

"Sorry, can't we talk tomorrow, senpai? I'm tired," I said.

"Hey! What's with that reaction? Aren't you supposed to shout, 'What are you doing here Suzune-senpai!'?"

"Er, yeah, I just call you senpai. Not Suzune-senpai. Anyway, I'm sure you noticed that Kazuki was acting strangely," I said.

Was she really there the whole time? She should've shown herself at the start! Well, I guess she was being considerate in her own twisted way.

"W-What's this? Why are you being so stoic, Usato-kun? Are you angry at me? Tell me why, and I'll fix it right away!" she pleaded.

"Why do you sound so desperate? And shouldn't you be getting back to the castle, senpai?" I inquired.

"Keep being so cold and you might make me cry," she said.

"Funny," I said flatly.

I couldn't imagine her crying. If she actually cried, I'd consider prostrating on the ground and begging her for forgiveness. But it seemed that she was too busy *saying* she'd cry to actually do it. She positioned herself next to me and looked up at the moon.

"Looks like Kazuki-kun's also made up his mind," she noted.

"To be honest, I was almost going to tell him that I didn't want him to fight," I said.

If he didn't want to fight, he didn't have to. If it only made him depressed, he shouldn't have to force himself to put his own life at risk. I looked in the direction that Kazuki had been running, then Inukami put her hands on my shoulders and faced me.

"Usato-kun . . . you don't want *me* to fight, do you?" she asked.

"Of course I don't. But you're different from Kazuki," I stated.

"Well, I can't deny that," she replied.

Kazuki was struggling in this world, but Inukami had no intention of going back home. Their thoughts and goals were totally different. Besides, even if I'd told her not to fight, I knew that I couldn't change her mind.

"You're my senpai. Don't say things that'll make me worry so much," I said.

"Ugh. Senpais have nothing to do with this world!" she exclaimed.

"Kazuki's my classmate and friend," I replied.

"Then I'm your friend too!" she countered.

"Yup," I answered.

"Okay, aren't you being a bit *too* casual now?!" she said.

I turned away from Inukami, who was mere centimeters from my face, and began walking toward the quarters. When I turned back to her, she was still standing there with her head hanging low. I was probably too mean to her. I figured I should probably make sure she was okay. If I didn't, something bad was likely to happen.

"But . . ." I started.

Inukami interrupted me. "It's too hard to ambush you, Usato-kun. Being a little more loving wouldn't kill you. Oh, wait. Were you about to say something just now?" she asked.

"It's nothing," I said.

"O-Oh . . . okay. I should get back to the castle. Good night, Usato-kun," she replied.

After a pause, I answered, "Good night."

What does Inukami want to do to me? It's a little . . . concerning.

*   *   *

The next morning, the king informed the public about the enemy's invasion, and soon enough word spread to the far reaches of the kingdom. The soldiers nervously braced themselves and the townspeople started to panic.

Earlier that morning, Rose had told me that the king's strategy was to march soldiers to the grasslands to launch an attack. Heroes Kazuki and Inukami were to lead the charge at the Kingdom Army Commander Siglis' behest.

After the king had made his announcement, Rose gathered the rescue team members in the dining hall. Ururu was looking fondly around the room; it was almost as if she hadn't seen it in ages. When she saw me, she smiled sweetly and waved at me for a second. I didn't know what to do in return.

"It's been a while, fellas," Ururu said.

Judging from the casual tone of her voice, I could only assume that the burly men didn't scare her. Any normal girl who saw them would run away screaming, but Ururu was apparently different. Not only did she have guts—when she reunited with the guys, it was like she was a different person.

"Looks like everyone's here. I'll get straight to the point," Rose started.

This was most likely about the forthcoming war. If my guess was correct, Orga and Ururu had only heard about the invasion when the king announced it earlier in the day.

"As you all know, the Demon Lord's army is coming. Actually, they're frantically rebuilding their bridge. But even so, they're still on their way here," Rose said.

She's speaking as if she wasn't the one that destroyed it. How does one person destroy an entire bridge anyway?

"In two days, the kingdom's army will march to the grasslands. The rescue team will join them and build an encampment on the land," she announced.

Orga and Ururu responded with, "Yes, ma'am," but Tong and the others answered back with an "Oorah!" Saying the guys answered strangely would be an understatement. They nearly drowned out what the siblings had said.

"This is Usato and Ururu's first war. Don't let your guard down," she warned.

But wait . . . if this is Ururu's first war, does that mean Orga was the only one who healed the wounded in the rear? That's a big job for one person.

Rose finished briefing us and the group went their separate ways. When some of us walked out of the dining hall, Rose called out, "Hey, Orga. Come here for a second."

"Understood," he said politely.

Rose seemed troubled, so I hurriedly took one step forward . . . only for Ururu to grab my arm out of nowhere. When I turned around, a wide smile played across her face.

"C-Can I help you?" I asked.

"I'm booored," she said.

"What about it?" I responded.

"I heard that you run around town with a Blue Grizzly cub," she noted.

"And?" I replied.

"Can I see it? Pretty pleeease?" she begged.

"Um . . ." I was at a loss for words.

"I bet he's adorable," she said.

"I don't know. He's pretty vicious," I responded.

She glared at me silently.

"Right this way!" I exclaimed.

"Thanks!" she replied.

I'm such a damn softie! If it were senpai, I could've subtly changed the subject and that would be that. But not this girl! She's something else! They're both the same age so why are they so dang different?! Gah! Ururu's a toughie.

Ururu happily accompanied me to Blurin's stable.

There he was in all his glory—yawning on the ground, looking like he didn't have a care in the world. He was a little bigger than he was the last time I saw him. If nothing else, it was proof that I needed to make him get proper exercise.

Ururu was staring at Blurin with a twinkle in her eye. Suddenly, she leaped at the bear with open arms and squealed, "It's SO cute!"

"Gah! Stay back!" I exclaimed.

But this wasn't Inukami, who usually had weird ulterior motives. I was sure that if Ururu had wholesome intentions, Blurin would let her pet him like he did with me and the gate-keeper (and Rose).

The next thing I heard was a roar, which was followed by a high-pitched squeal.

"Ururu-san?!" I shouted.

It turned out that Blurin had used all his strength to jump up and swat Ururu down like a fly, which left her in a giant pile of hay. It was the first time I'd seen Blurin slam dunk a person. I frantically pulled Ururu out of the hay only for her to grab my shoulders with a dumbfounded look on her face. Blurin must have gone easy on her because she wasn't hurt, but I could have sworn that I saw a tear in her eye.

"Usato-kun," she said.

"Y-Yes?" I asked.

"You pet him," she demanded.

"Okay. But first, you're gonna have to let go of my shoulders," I replied.

Her nails were digging into my skin, and it *hurt*. She probably couldn't stand being rejected. Following Ururu's orders, I petted Blurin on the head like I normally did.

"See?" I said.

"Th-Then I can try too!" she exclaimed.

But Blurin simply roared and immediately slapped her right

hand. Tears welled up in Ururu's eyes as she blankly stared at her hand. With no soft fur to pet, she lightly scratched the back of her head, attempting to distract me from her tears. As I stood there feeling sorry for her, I saw a small, familiar black creature jump onto the downtrodden girl's shoulders.

"Kukuru-chan . . ." Ururu said.

The rabbit squeaked in response.

It was Kukuru, Rose's loyal pet—the monster who toyed with my pure boyish heart! Surprised by this unexpected appearance, Ururu looked at the rabbit and smiled.

"Are you . . . comforting me?" Ururu said. She tried to rub her cheek against the rabbit. Th-Thank . . ."

But Kukuru quickly jumped from Ururu's shoulder to mine.

". . .Oh," Ururu said.

I was petting Blurin with my right hand, I had Kukuru on my left shoulder, and in front of me was Ururu, whose jaw had basically dropped to the floor. Silence pervaded the area.

Both animals happily started cooing, but they really should have shut up! Waterworks were bound to start any second!

I hurriedly wrapped both hands around the rabbit and thrust it toward Ururu. When I saw that she was holding it, I let out a sigh of relief and tried to get the heck out of the stable.

"Y-Yeah, Blurin's kinda cranky today! Anyway, let's head outside," I said.

Without responding, Ururu silently left the stable with Kukuru in hand. I started walking toward the quarters because silent Ururu was freaking me out. She was acting totally different than she did at the stable.

"Hey, Usato-kun?" she said.

"Eek!" I said, my voice cracking. "I-I mean, yeah?"

"Rose-san is scary," she stated.

"Isn't that blatantly obvious?" I countered.

"Ooh, look who's got a sharp tongue. Anyway, when we first joined the rescue team, she really monitored our training. It was kind of obsessive," she explained.

"In what way?" I asked.

"She was super strict. The rescue team was still very new back then, but the training was so harsh that most people would escape because they just couldn't take it," she said.

It wasn't hard to imagine. Before I grew thicker skin, Rose's exercises were mentally and physically draining. It was only natural that people would flee if they couldn't keep up.

"Why did you and your brother join the rescue team?" I inquired.

"Because Rose invited us. We ended up only providing support. But in the beginning, she was our direct superior. To be honest, that made me so happy," she said.

Happy, huh? I never would have guessed. Things must've gone downhill from there.

"But I just didn't have what it takes. Sure, there were times where I couldn't keep up with my brother, but it mainly didn't work out because I was scared of Rose," she admitted.

"And she's still as scary as ever," I joked.

"That may be true, but she was much scarier then. In fact, nowadays Rose-san actually looks kinda happy," she said.

Why is she happy? Is it because I'm a new sandbag that she can beat silly? That doesn't make **me** *happy, but I can only speak for myself.*

"I think she believes in you, Usato-kun," she continued.

"Believes in me? Come on, that's taking it a little too far," I smirked.

"No, I mean it," she said with a serious look on her face. "Don't hate her, Usato-kun. As scary as she is, she's a really good person."

It was the same thing that Orga had said to me the other day. It surprised me that both siblings relayed the same message, but either way my response was the same.

"Believe me, I never hated her and I never will," I answered.

Ururu smiled in response, but I didn't know why. We kept talking until we arrived at the entrance to the quarters. She put Kukuru down at the entrance and faced me.

"You know what I think, Usato-kun? I think her feelings are easily hurt," she said.

"Yeah, right," I answered.

Ururu laughed. "I wouldn't be so sure, you know. Really!"

What does she mean by "easily hurt"?

"Most of the time that lady's freaking unhinged! She's been kinda nice recently, but she's usually not like that at all!" I exclaimed.

"H-Hey . . . Usato-kun?" Ururu started.

But I was ready to rant.

"You have no idea how much I went through when she threw me into the forest! I mean, it was kind of cool that she never left, but that's that, and this is another matter entirely! I seriously thought I was going to die! And when she told me that she's twenty-five, I was shocked! She looks so much older than that!" I shouted

"My deepest apologies, Usato-kun," Ururu whispered.

I had no idea why she was apologizing until . . .

I was in so much pain I was screaming!

"Like to run your mouth, dontcha? You won't be talkin' when I'm done with you," said a voice.

At that moment, Rose sunk her fingers into my skull and lifted me off the ground by my head, which left me writhing in pain. I caught a glimpse of Rose, who apparently had been standing behind me, with Kukuru sitting on her shoulder. This could only mean that the dang rabbit got me in trouble again!

I was in too much pain to speak.

"Don't be so hard on him," Ururu suggested.

"This kid leaves me no choice," replied Rose. "Orga's

waiting inside. I basically told him everything you need to know, so go hear it from him," Rose commanded.

"Will do! See ya later, Usato-kun," Ururu said.

Ururu threw me to the wolves! How could she?!

Rose released me from her iron grip, then started carrying me to the quarters as a vein popped angrily out of her head. I was too weak to move.

She acts like I'm so easy to carry. Well, whatever. She can do whatever she wants.

CHAPTER 7

As a Member of the Rescue Team!

Everyone on the rescue team was riding a horse-drawn carriage to the grasslands. I sat next to Rose as she steered the horses, while Orga and Ururu sat inside the carriage with the other scary-looking team members. The knights of Llinger Kingdom marched in a line in front of the carriage.

"Um, why am I sitting next to you, Captain?" I asked.

"Only 'cause there's no room inside. Or did you want to be the only one walkin'?" she smirked.

"Not really," I answered.

Sitting in that cramped carriage with the guys would have been awkward. But dealing with a dead silent Rose wasn't fun either. I would've gone mad if I had to sit in silence for hours, so I decided to ask her a question that had been on my mind.

"This is your second time fighting the Demon Lord's army, right, Captain? What are demons like in general? All I know is that they're different from humans," I said.

"Demons are demihumans who have twisted horns on their heads. They look similar to humans, but they typically out-match us in strength and magic power," she explained.

"Did you just say horns?" I inquired.

Like the horns of the devil?

"Why? You scared?" she said.

"Nah. I know someone who's scarier, so I'll be okay."

Rose scoffed. "The kid's got a comment for everything."

I can see why she views me as a kid . . . since she's an old hag and all.

I didn't want her to slaughter me, so I kept that remark to myself.

"If you're still nervous after all of my training, I'm gonna kick you right off of this carriage," she said playfully, tugging tightly on the reins. "Who woulda thought that the kid who was dragged into the hero summoning would turn into such a monster," she mused.

"A monster? You don't have to phrase it so weirdly," I said.

It's not like I'm inhuman, you know.

"But it's true. Normal people can't handle my training," she remarked.

"Then why did you make it so hard to endure?!" I said.

"You're the monster who cleared my training, so anything you say just sounds sarcastic," she countered.

If she knows what she's doing, that's downright cruel!

"*You're* the monster!" I said.

"Excuse me?"

"Sorry. I didn't mean it."

She wouldn't even let me talk back. I felt really pathetic. One evil glare had me apologizing to Rose.

"Well, in any case, I'm glad I found you when I did," she replied.

Wait, really?

"What? Why do you look so surprised?" she asked.

"I didn't expect that at all," I said honestly.

I never thought she'd say that she's glad that we met.

"You have no idea how special you are," she responded.

"What do you mean?"

"There aren't any healers like me in this world. I can train the healers in the carriage all I want, but nothing would change."

She was right. No matter how hard Orga and Ururu trained, they could never become a healer like Rose. Was she saying that I was like her, which is why I was special? I didn't really know how to feel.

"Imagine if there were a whole bunch of people who were just like me," she said.

"That would surely be the end of the world."

She karate chopped me in the stomach so fast that I had no time to react. Air spilled out of my mouth, and I started to faint. Rose simply sat there with her hand to her head, looking nonplussed.

"It ain't gonna happen. That's why I found a way to use healing magic to train past my limits. You and me are the only ones who can do it," she said.

I wheezed in pain as I cast healing magic on my stomach. "M-Makes sense . . ."

But I was surprised to hear that she'd come up with . . . this novel way to use healing magic. Her "ideas" were pretty insane.

"You had the capabilities I was looking for in a healer. No one could do what I did . . . until I found you," she murmured.

I wasn't sure what Rose meant, but I did know that Ururu was right. Rose really was counting on me. Despite all the pain I had suffered, I couldn't help but feel kind of honored.

I was still thinking about our conversation when she turned to me and said, "Almost there." When I snapped out of my daze, the trees on both sides of the road had faded away, leaving nothing but a giant green field.

*   *   *

Three days had passed since the bridge was destroyed.

Amila Vergrett angrily gritted her teeth as she reflected on the unfortunate turn of events. The bridge had been so close to completion, but then it was destroyed in an instant. The army had to rebuild it from scratch.

"Tch. How much longer will it take?!" Amila growled.

"It should be completed by daybreak," a subordinate answered.

"Well, hurry up!" she yelled.

She had committed the biggest blunder there was. If she had just kept an eye on the shore, the bridge would have never been destroyed. Amila was angry at herself for making such a rookie mistake.

"Morale's lower than ever and the attack is terribly delayed. I don't deserve the title of third army commander," she lamented.

A knight in black armor approached Amila. "It's still not completed? I'm bored to tears," he grumbled.

"Well hold your horses," she said weakly. "When the battle commences, you'll have to fight whether you like it or not."

The black knight morosely sat on the ground. "I don't care as long as I get to fight."

"Quite the battle junkie, aren't you? I would've never guessed you were the subordinate of that lamebrained freak of nature," said Amila.

"I've got nothing to do with that slacker," he hissed.

The black knight didn't take orders from the third division, which was led by Amila. Instead, he was sent there as a soldier from the second division. Amila was painfully aware that the second army commander didn't take his job seriously, and as a fellow commander, she couldn't respect him. However, his subordinate—the black knight—was clearly skilled. There were rumors that none of his fellow soldiers could match his incredible strength and unique magic abilities.

"Listen, I know you're talented. But don't let your guard down. The humans have their own tricks up their sleeves. We call them the kidnappers," she explained.

"You mean the guys who take fallen soldiers off the field?

If all they do is flee, they can never defeat me," he replied.

"Don't underestimate them just because they're human. They're their own type of monster," Amila warned. Despite how serious she was being, the black knight apathetically shrugged in response.

Amila saw this and let out a sigh. "No matter. Tomorrow we finish the bridge. After that, we start our assault. You and Baljinak will be responsible for exterminating our enemies. Morale's at an all-time low. It's your job to boost it," she noted.

Amila quickly walked away from the black knight in a not-so-subtle attempt to end the conversation and went back to directing construction. The black knight stared at the back of Amila's head before collapsing onto the floor.

"Monsters, huh?" he moaned. He drew his sword and tossed it onto the ground. If Amila saw him recklessly throw a sword—a symbol of pride for the knights—she would have been furious.

"I don't know how strong they are, but at least I'll get to have a little fun," he mumbled. The black armor he wore started twisting and turning like the haze of heat on a scorching hot day.

"Demons or humans . . . It doesn't matter. Anyone who can satisfy me will do," he groaned. He started maniacally laughing, his mouth hidden under his helmet.

"Show me how it feels to live, humans," he said.

His jet-black armor squirmed around him like sludge.
He looked like the devil himself.

* * *

The kingdom's army set up an encampment on the vast field. But in a separate area, the rescue team pitched a large tent-like structure that had its own roof. We lined it with simple beds that we'd packed in the carriage.

The sun had already set. Soldiers stood guard, relieving each other in shifts, while I sat in a wooden chair in the rescue team's camp. The chair was absurdly uncomfortable, but the biggest problem was . . .

"There's nothing to do," I groaned.

Rose was with Siglis, and the siblings had left to talk with the soldiers. On top of that, Tong's group was already asleep.

The Demon Lord's army might be here any minute, so how in the world are they sleeping like babies?! "Resting helps us fight better," they say? Sounds pretty bogus to me.

Rose had also told me to rest, but I wasn't sure if I should. If I were on Earth, however, I would sleep in a heartbeat.

"Coming through!" said a brash voice.

The gatekeeper who'd accompanied me and Inukami burst into the tent. The only difference was that now he was wearing the kingdom's army uniform.

After we greeted each other, he surveyed the room.

"Glad to see you, Sir Usato. Where are the others?" he asked.

"They're out at the moment. The captain should be back pretty soon," I said.

"Well, you see, the reason I'm here is because I have a message for you," he replied. He straightened his posture and bowed once again. "I am Aruku! And I have the honor of guarding the rescue team in this battle! I will protect your team to the end!" he exclaimed.

"G-Great. I look forward to working with you, Aruku-san," I responded.

His impassioned words surprised me a little, but they also reminded me that his intensions were pure. The enemy would probably make a beeline for our camp, so I had hoped that someone trustworthy—someone like him—would defend us. I could rest easy knowing that he had our backs.

"Leave it to me! Now, sir, I'll return to my post!" he exclaimed.

"We're counting on you," I said.

After bowing politely once more, Aruku exited the tent.

He was an incredibly enthusiastic person whose cheerful attitude lit up the room. I watched Aruku walk away, then returned to my chair and stared out into space. Just then, a girl entered the tent. She had long, beautiful black hair that swayed as she walked. It was none other than Inukami who approached me with a smile.

"How's it going, Usato-kun?" she said.

She wore gleaming silver armor. It looked fairly light and easy to move in. Inukami proudly puffed out her chest when she noticed that I was looking at her.

"Oh, this? It's . . . Well, should I tell you? Wanna know what it is?" she giggled.

"Not really," I said honestly.

"Sure you do, so listen up! I'll explain it just for you!" she exclaimed.

She's gonna tell me, whether I like it or not!

"Support magic has been cast on this armor! It specifically bolsters my lightning magic. Not only that, but it's so flexible that I forget that it's there! It's amazing!" she shouted.

"You like it?" I responded.

"Oh, absolutely!" she said.

She's beyond easy to read. She's like a child who's proud of her new toy. I mean in the sense that it's kind of annoying.

"You're not very girly, senpai," I noted.

"What the—?! You've got some nerve saying that to a girl!" she said.

"Well, you're the only girl I know who's happy to have her own armor," I replied.

"Th-That's not true, Usato-kun! I like cute things and don't you forget it! In fact, I used to have a cactus in my room back on Earth!" she said.

Does owning a cactus really make someone girly?

I glared at senpai for a few seconds until she awkwardly averted her eyes.

She suddenly started pointing at me. "Yeah, well. *You're* the one who stole everything that made me feel better!" she shouted.

"What? I did?!" I said.

Now she's just trying to pick a fight.

"That's why you've got to make me feel better yourself!" she reasoned.

"Sorry, I have no idea what you're talking about. That makes no sense," I replied.

She started inching toward me. It creeped me out, so I slowly rose out of my chair.

"You're stubborn, Usato-kun, but I'm not gonna give up!" she announced.

"I never gave you a reason to try in the first place," I responded.

She giggled. "I know what this is. This is your way of hiding your embarrassment. Of pretending you're more aloof than you are!" she exclaimed.

Inukami was acting really strange. She was even going cross-eyed.

"Calm down, senpai. You're being weird," I said.

"No, I'm not!" she countered.

"Um, are you okay?" I asked.

Crap. She's really gone off the deep end.

Inukami was a regular high school girl back on Earth. She was trying to be brave, but deep down she was probably scared. The pressure from the war must have made her unstable. Maybe that was why she was acting so manic.

"Just hear me out! When you resist me, it just makes me want you even more. It makes me want to flirt and be flirted with. So, let's do it!" she cried.

"Actually, I was wrong," I said. "You were always a weirdo."

By "getting closer" does she mean . . .

"I get it, I get it, already. So, let's just stop it right here. People are supposed to talk to each other. Why don't we have a normal, two-way conversation?" I asked, trembling.

I slowly started backing away. After what I'd just said, I was sure that she would calm down and talk to me normally. She looked like she was considering my proposition, but then . . .

"Sometimes we have to do manual labor," she said ominously. "This happens to be one of those times."

"Kazukiiiiiiii! Heeeeeeelp!" I shouted.

If you can hear me Kazuki, my best friend in the world, I need you to save me!

Just then, Kazuki burst into the tent. He was wearing thick armor, unlike Inukami, and looked truly concerned.

"What's wrong, Usato?!" Kazuki shouted.

"You came!" I exclaimed. I couldn't believe how fast he'd arrived.

When Kazuki spotted Inukami, he started pointing at her.

"So that's where you are, senpai! I was looking all over for you! Siglis-san wants to have a tactical meeting. Let's go," he explained.

"Don't worry, I'll be there as soon as Usato-kun falls into the palm of my hand," she answered.

"Um, what do you mean?" Kazuki asked nervously.

"You two have deepened your relationship. That's what I'm talking about," she said.

Sorry, but . . . please stop talking nonsense. We don't know what that means.

Kazuki looked at her like she had twenty heads.

"Inukami-senpai's going insane! Take her away, Kazuki!" I shouted.

"I-I don't know what's going on, but I believe you, Usato!" he cried.

Kazuki locked her in a full nelson and began dragging her out of the tent.

"I knew it! It's you! You're stopping me from getting close to Usato-kun! You made sure that you guys became better friends only to leave your senpai out in the cold! That's so underhanded, Kazuki-kun!" she growled.

"What are you talking about?!" Kazuki asked.

I feel the same way, Kazuki. I have no idea what she is saying.

"Let me go!" she yelled.

"S-See you later, Usato!" Kazuki called out.

"Seriously, thank you so much!" I called back.

Inukami left the tent like a tornado, nearly destroying everything in her path. She wasn't a bad person, and we definitely got along, so overall I was glad we were friends.

But why me? I didn't know why she liked me. If this were a dating sim, I had no recollection of picking her route. I didn't have the social skills or swag to make a girl swoon in the first place.

"Hmm . . . I don't get it," I whispered.

But I really didn't have time to think about romance. Until the scouts returned to camp, there was no telling when the battle would start.

"I've just gotta brace myself before then," I said.

*   *   *

The next morning, I found myself gazing at the vast field. My right hand trembled as I reached for the sword that King Lloyd had given to me.

"It's okay. It's okay," I said quietly. I was trying to calm myself down.

The battle would start as soon as the enemy's shadow fell on the land. Me and senpai were heroes, and our job was to blast enemy soldiers with magic, to create a path to the demon commander with our allies, and to *hopefully* put the Demon Lord's reign to an end.

I wasn't sure it was possible, but we had to try.

"Don't overexert yourself, Kazuki-kun," said senpai, standing next to me as she uttered those caring words.

"I'll be okay. No need to worry about me," I said.

"You say that, but . . ." she trailed off.

"You're the nervous one, senpai. So nervous, in fact, that you tried distracting yourself in the tent with Usato," I retorted.

She angrily pursed her lips and looked away as if I'd hit the nail on the head. I'd never seen her make that face back on Earth. We spent a lot of time working together on the student council, so I knew her well. At the very least, she'd never act so vulnerable in front of a total stranger.

"You know people pretty well. Of course, I feel nervous. But honestly, it's also kind of exciting," she admitted.

I knew what she meant. Wielding sturdy armor and a sword, I would take to the front lines, which would instantly etch me into this world's history as a hero. In that sense, I could see why Inukami was excited. But in my case . . .

"I'm fighting for a different reason, senpai," I said.

The reason I was fighting wasn't for fame or recognition. It was to save my dear friends Usato and Inukami.

She chuckled. "I bet. But this is just who I am."

"You're a lot different than you were back home, senpai," I replied.

"It's true. But the old Inukami is dead. Despite that, Usato has always stuck by my side. I now know what path I want to take in my life," she stated.

Something must have happened between Inukami and Usato while I wasn't around. I looked curiously at Inukami.

"Back when we went missing—actually, never mind. I'll tell you later. If we make it home in one piece, I'll tell you what happened," she said as a smile spread across her face.

"*If?* Why not *when?*" I asked.

"Is there a reason you *have* to go home?" she asked, still smiling.

Inukami was the only girl I knew who could smile in such dire straits. If I was being mean about it, I would say that she wasn't nervous enough. But on the other hand, I found her relaxed attitude reassuring. While we were throwing quips back and forth, a disturbingly ominous feeling swept over my body.

Without so much as a thought, I glanced at the grasslands. The Demon Lord's army wasn't here, but they were approaching. Inukami also gazed nervously at the field. Amid a somewhat eerie silence, my heart started to sting.

"Senpai!" I shouted.

"They're here!" she exclaimed.

Siglis must have noticed them, too.

All kinds of orders were dispatched to the troops. A knight who specialized in magic headed to the front lines, just like Siglis had planned.

"We've got to get ready," Inukami said.

"I know!" I replied. I took slow, deep breaths and boosted my magic.

I possessed light magic. I didn't know how effective it would be against the enemy army, but there was only one way to find out. I was getting used to the feeling of power running through my body. As I'd expected, getting used to feeling magic wasn't so easy.

"The kingdom's army shall fight till we destroy the Demon Lord's army!" yelled Siglis from the rear. He was shouting to heighten the soldiers' morale. The soldiers' eyes gleamed. They were ready for battle.

"We fight for the King! For the people! For Llinger Kingdom!" he shouted.

The fear dissipated from all the soldiers' eyes as they raised their voices to cheer. It was an incredible sight to behold; they were yelling so loud that the ground beneath us was practically shaking. As the troops roared in response, a black shadow stained a hill on the field. The shadow was small, since it was so far away, but it looked like a black blob of darkness.

"What *is* that?" I mused.

Suddenly, shadows descended on the hill like an avalanche. The beings looked somewhat human except for the sharp, pointed horns on their heads.

"Prepare the magic troops!" Siglis commanded.

I yelped when I heard his voice; it brought my thoughts back to the battlefield. I glanced back at the Demon Lord's army as they sped down the hill.

"We'll strike first. Can you do it?" Inukami asked.

"I can and I will! I'll give it everything I've got!" I said.

I held out my hands and gathered all my magic into my palms. The magic knights were on standby on the front lines, holding out their hands just like me and Inukami. We were prepared to blast the enemy with magic the moment they were in range.

"Gotta go all-out on the first attack!" Inukami exclaimed.

Sparks flew off her body in every direction. We were both prepared to attack, but the Demon Lord's army did not stop their charge. They were so reckless that it almost seemed like a suicide mission.

"When I give the signal, we fire!" Siglis shouted.

The distance was closing between the two armies. There was no backing out now. I gritted my teeth, opened my eyes wide, and . . .

"Fiiiiiiire!" Siglis shouted.

I yelled as I launched shining, white magic straight ahead.

A few moments later, all sorts of magic rained down on the enemy.

*   *   *

A terrifying explosion ripped through the sky.

"It begins," I whispered.

All of us on the rescue team were lined up in front of Rose.

"If you're wearing black, you will first head to the field and retrieve any wounded soldiers you find," Rose explained.

The thugs in black gave a hearty, "Oorah!"

Is it just me, or do their clothes seem a little bit off? Wearing black jackets on the battlefield makes them look much more like criminals than anything else. Honestly, if one of them got a hold of me, I'd probably cry.

"You two in gray will do your job here. If there's an emergency, leave at once," she commanded.

Orga and Ururu answered, "Yes, ma'am!" Their clothes looked like mine and Rose's, except theirs were gray. It was their duty to hold down the fort.

"Lastly, you and me are gonna weave through the field and breach the front lines," she stated.

"Understood," I said.

"All right!" she shouted. "Tong, Alec, Mill, Gomul, and Gurd. Head out!"

All the thugs raised their voices at once.

"Heh. Then get going. Do what you did last time and come back alive!" she said.

No need to worry about them. They've got so much endurance it's scary!

The thugs noisily sped out of the room. The rest of us watched them leave from inside the tent.

"I hope senpai and Kazuki are all right," I murmured as I stared at the exit.

"Are you worried about your friends?" Ururu suddenly asked.

"Of course," I replied instantly.

"I see," she said. "You've gotta be careful out there too, Usato-kun."

"Yeah, I know," I responded.

While Ururu and I were talking, Tong rushed into the tent. He was carrying a weeping female knight over his soldier.

"I got one!" Tong announced.

"Already?!" Ururu and I said at the same time.

How?! The battle just started!

"Well, yeah. It's normal for people to get hurt when there is a war. They're gonna start bringing more in—a whole bunch of 'em. Tong, leave her to Usato and bring us the next wounded soldier," Rose demanded.

"I gotcha, big sis! Hey Usato, I'm countin' on ya!" said Tong.

"R-Right," I said nervously. He handed me the female knight.

There were deep gashes in her legs and her shoulders that came from a sword. She was bleeding a lot, but a wound like this was easy to cure.

"Urk . . . he had such . . . a scary face," she whimpered.

"You poor thing," I said, feeling genuinely sorry for her. "You must have been crying because of how much it hurt. Yeah, that must be it. But I promise it'll all be okay. We'll make the pain go away. Look at me and the lady right here. No more freakish thugs. I promise!"

"Usato-kun, don't lose sight of your mission," Rose warned.

Oh. I guess she can hear me.

I let go of the knight to pour healing magic into her wounds, but for some reason she kept clinging to me. It only took a few seconds to heal her.

"Are you okay?" I asked the flustered knight.

"A big monster . . . and an enemy in black . . ." she stammered.

"Please try to calm down," I urged. She was too scared to recall what had happened.

An enemy in black, she says.

Throbbing pain ran through my head and the beastkin girl's vision replayed in my mind. I didn't know why I saw it at first, but then I finally understood what it meant.

"This must mean that Kazuki and senpai are really going to die."

*   *   *

The kingdom's army tried to massacre us with long-range magic, but we outsmarted them—we used large-scale illusion magic to deceive them. Under the influence of illusion magic, the knights would surely misdirect their shots, which would then cause them to panic. That was when I planned to take the demon-made monster Baljinak to the front lines and launch an attack.

"Humans. So weak," I muttered.

One kingdom knight lay face down on the ground. He was groaning in pain as blood spilled out of his stomach. He didn't know what I had just done to him.

"What . . . is this? Who the hell are you?" he asked, glaring at me.

"Welp. I guess you'll never know," I answered flippantly.

I stepped over the poor bastard to look for my next target.

That was when something struck me as odd. I was knee-deep in an ocean of the enemy's blood. It seemed that I had wiped out all of the kingdom's knights in the area. Slaughtering them was so easy that I didn't realize I'd done it.

"What a bore," I said. "Humans are too easy to kill."

I languidly lowered my sword and started walking, albeit haphazardly, toward the enemy. Out of the corner of my eye, I saw Baljinak. The massive creature sent the kingdom's knights flying before it eventually crushed them to death.

"Did they really need my help? With *this*?" I muttered.

No matter how I looked at it, our army was stronger than theirs. Our soldiers were struggling, but they were still striking the enemy down one by one. I couldn't understand why in the previous battle we had just ran away.

I was so lost in thought that I didn't notice that another knight was running at me with his sword. "How dare you kill my brothers!" he shrieked.

Before I could hit him, the enemy plunged his sword into my armor.

"Got him!" he shouted.

You must have felt the sword hit me. Sorry, but you didn't "get" me. Looks like you were dead wrong.

"I pity you. I really do," I said.

"What?!" the knight yelled.

I smirked as I put my magic to work. The knight, puzzled by a strange feeling, started vomiting blood.

"Guh . . . Does this mean . . . we're all . . ." the knight trailed off.

After that, he dropped his sword and fell flat on his back. To add insult to injury, I stabbed the knight and dragged the blade from his shoulder down to his spleen. The blood he had vomited dyed his armor dark red.

I took the knight's sword out of my body. My armor writhed as if it had a life of its own, then instantly closed the gaping wound from the sword. In the end, human efforts were worthless. When faced with inevitable doom, all humans did was throw countless men into battle.

Suddenly, the knight who had vomited blood started groaning.

"What? Still alive?" I inquired.

"If I don't tell them now . . . they'll . . ." he trailed off.

"You're a stubborn one, I'll give you that," I replied.

His vacant eyes searched for his comrades. He probably couldn't see where he was anymore. As I watched the knight crawl toward his men, I decided to put him out of his misery.

But before I got to do that, I caught a glimpse of a black figure.

So, I stopped mid-swing and whipped my sword about to slice whatever it was, but I didn't hit anything. I looked around but all I saw was my comrades and enemy knights fighting.

"Maybe I'm just seeing things," I murmured.

I turned back to the dying man and raised my sword to finish him off once again, but then I noticed something.

The knight I had stepped over, the one that was lying face down, was nowhere in sight!

Did he crawl away while I wasn't looking? That's impossible. The wound was too deep. He couldn't have moved that fast.

"What just happened?" I mumbled.

I looked around once more, surveying the area. Nothing. So, I turned my attention back down again to finish off the groaning knight. But I was astonished to find that he had also seemingly vanished! I couldn't help but wonder if this was part of the enemy army's magic. Or perhaps this was what Amila had meant.

"It's the monsters," I said.

It must have been the kidnappers—the nonviolent soldiers who ran through the battlefield. I started laughing harder than I'd ever laughed in my life. It was just as she'd said! Those ridiculous humans were actually here!

Unable to contain my giddiness, I howled with laughter as I stood on the battlefield. My armor squirmed wildly as if it were trying to express my emotions. When I calmed down, my armor returned to its usual state, and I started walking again.

The war wasn't over just yet. There was someone stronger out there—a human who would give me the thrill I was seeking. Just the thought of it kept me laughing like crazy.

Funnily enough, something else caught my eye, A short distance away, I saw a bright light and lightning, which blasted through the air with a deafening roar. These two types of magic were especially strong.

"This looks like fun," I stated. I broke into a smile and headed toward it. I couldn't wait to toy with the enemy.

* * *

I had healed so many people since the battle started that I was starting to lose count. Wounded soldiers were being rushed in and out of the tent. I was in the middle of healing when Rose suddenly mumbled, "It's time."

Orga looked concerned. "Will you be leaving, Rose-san?"

"You idiot," she said, "when we're here, you know damn well to call me Captain."

It took me a few moments to understand what she'd meant: I would have to join her in battle. I had more than enough magic at my disposal. My uniform was as white and as clean as it was on the day that I'd received it.

"It's showtime, Usato. You ready?" Rose said. Her smile was even fiercer than usual.

"Of course. You trained me to be your right-hand man, and I'm ready," I replied.

"Yeah. Good to hear. Almost forgot you're a go-getter. Looks like I was worried for nothin'," she grinned.

"Were you worried about me?" I asked. "I had no idea."

"Hah! Always have a comeback now, don't ya? Orga, Uru-ru, hold down the fort. If enemies ambush the tent, I want you to run for the hills," Rose commanded.

This was important for the siblings in the rear to remember. They weren't very strong, so the best thing they could do in a fight was run like hell. If something were to happen to them, the wounded would go unhealed.

"Understood. Don't worry about us. Just focus on saving as many people as you can," Orga replied.

"Don't get hurt," Ururu said.

Rose simply replied, "Thanks." She turned away from them and nonchalantly waved goodbye. It looked casual, but I could tell that it was full of emotion.

"Orga-san, Ururu-san. I don't want this to be our last goodbye. I'll do everything in my power to make sure that doesn't happen," I said reassuringly.

"Take care," Orga said.

Ururu also chimed in. "If it's too dangerous, you can always run away, Usato-kun. Please come back safely."

After we said our farewells, I attempted to catch up to Rose.

"Hurry up," she barked.

I silently complied and followed her outside the tent. When I emerged from the tent, Aruku showered me with words of encouragement and told me how our soldiers were faring. The enemy had pushed through a good deal of the army, but even so our men were standing their ground.

Sweat dripped from my forehead as I walked behind Rose. Suddenly, she turned to me. "I've got one last word of advice," she noted.

"Yes?" I asked curiously.

"You can't kill anyone, that right?" she inquired.

"Right. I mean, my duty is to save people, not kill them," I answered.

"If you spout that nonsense when they've got you surrounded, you'd be one stupid son of a bitch," she said.

That scenario hadn't even occurred to me. The plan was to instantly heal and flee if they attacked, but Rose wasn't satisfied with my strategy.

"Well, if you're gonna do somethin' stupid, I might as well teach you a technique I've been saving for a moment like this. I'm only gonna say it once, so listen up," she ordered.

"Yes, ma'am," I answered.

And with that, Rose told me about her technique. It was so mind-boggling that I honestly didn't know how to react. There was no good reason to use it, and even if I did it right, I would just end up fainting. But despite all that, I couldn't deny that it was the epitome of the wrong way to use healing magic.

"That technique's amazing" I murmured.

"Heh. Glad you agree," she answered.

"Wait. Did you create that technique just for me?" I asked.

"As if," she replied.

"In any case, thank you," I said.

She turned away from me and grunted, then looked straight ahead. "Tong told me something that sounds kinda suspicious," she mumbled.

"What's that?" I asked.

"It's about an enemy in black armor. His magic is dangerous, so better watch out," she noted.

"Black armor, huh?"

I grimaced.

The vision flashed in my head once more. In the worst-case scenario, Kazuki and Inukami would die. I shook my head in an attempt to shake off the image that was burned into my mind.

"You listening?" Rose growled.

"Oh, uh, y-yes, ma'am!" I answered.

It's too late to worry. We've got a battle to fight.

I took a deep breath, focused, and sharpened my senses. Now that my sense of hearing was heightened, sounds from the battlefield poured into my ears. I was more nervous than I'd ever been in my life. My body was tight with fear, but I couldn't stop my legs from marching onto the field.

"Let's go, Usato," Rose commanded.

I took a deep breath. If we were on the battlefield together, nothing could scare me.

"Yes, Captain!" I shouted.

The captain and I took off like a rocket.

As I ran toward the front lines, I caught a glance of Rose splitting off from me to cover other parts of the field. The overwhelming smell of iron—of spilled blood—filled my nose

as I breathed in the air. My eyes started to water from the un-
bearable stench, but I had to keep breathing if I wanted to get
used to it. I didn't come this far to let trivial things like this slow
me down.

I ignored the Demon Lord's soldiers that were coming my
way. There were wounded men on the field, but I was confident
that the other members would bring them back to the tent. I
was focused on cutting through the field to the front lines
ahead.

"So, this is the battlefield," I whispered.

This was the moment I'd been training for. I wouldn't let
the war take me down. I refused to stand frozen with fear. The
battle on the front lines was so brutal and bloody that healing
myself wasn't an option. Even so, I knew what I had to do next.

I spotted two wounded soldiers on the field and ran to
them with all the power I had in my legs. I was strong because
I'd trained my body. I saw fast-moving objects because I'd
trained in the forest. I zigzagged through the field because I'd
trained in town. All my fatigue would be healed by magic. My
healing magic couldn't be in better shape!

I sped through the field, weaving through allied and enemy
soldiers alike, and took the shortest route to a wounded person
on the ground. I swiftly lifted them up, only for them to say,
"Whaaat?! You're a healer?!"

The nearby demons swung their axes at me, but it was too late. They were so weak that any of the brawny rescue team members could've beaten them. Escaping the demons was as easy as pie.

My goal wasn't to strike down my enemies, but to rescue everyone that I could. I carried the wounded as I effortlessly dodged the enemy's axes. Ignoring all the enemies who tried to attack me, I scooped up a wounded soldier in my other arm without any trouble. After that, I sped off the field and retreated from the front lines.

The second person in my arm turned toward me. "Unh? Who? Who *are* you?"

They were conscious and their injuries could be easily healed in a matter of seconds. I had already finished healing the soldier in my other arm, and they were conscious as well. They were both proof that the soldiers fighting on the front lines possessed a frightening amount of strength and perseverance.

"I'm almost done healing you. Please stay still for a moment," I instructed.

After I stepped away from the front lines, I helped the two people back to their feet. They both stared at me in astonishment as they rubbed the spots I'd healed. There was no time to explain. I had to get back to the battle. Soldiers were fighting for their lives, and it was my job to save them.

"You're all healed. If you're still not feeling well, I advise you to stay away from the front lines," I said. After that, I ran to the front lines.

So long as I'm here, I'm not going to let anyone die.

EXTRA

Suzune's Journal

Before we battle the Demon Lord's army, I'd like to write down what I'm feeling right now. If I die in this war, I want you to read the rest of this journal. I'd like to tell you the story of Suzune Inukami—the girl who has now accepted her fate.

My life was terribly boring. Studies, sports, you name it—I mastered everything I set out to complete. I was blessed with a loving family and great friends at school. It was a picture-perfect life, but a painfully boring one, nonetheless.

I hated myself, so I asked other people about their futures. I didn't know what I wanted to do with my life and felt jealous when people told me their dreams.

I know it's ridiculous. I'm the one who stopped thinking for myself—who closed myself off from the world—because I thought that I could do anything. As it turns out, my attitude only tightened my shackles. I was the one who stopped fighting my fate, and yet there I was, distraught by the state of the world. I know it sounds silly, but that's how I felt.

I never wanted perfection. I just wanted a life that wasn't controlled by my parents, but that wasn't something they were willing to give me. I was born into a distinguished family that was chained to old, traditional values.

From a young age, I spent my days studying and taking various lessons in the hopes that I would live up to my parents' expectations. I was never allowed to play with my peers.

That was when it really hit me. Did I want to live my life as an obedient marionette to my parents? I was disappointed in myself for being perfect. It was clear that a monotonous existence was imminent. Before I came to this world, the thought of it plagued me every day.

Some people might say that I'm blessed. If they don't find being born to a distinguished family—and being shackled to a predictable life—boring, then you know what? Maybe they're right.

But that will not make me happy. The truth is . . . I hated it.

Usato-kun, Kazuki-kun, this next section's for you.

When I was first summoned to this world, the only person I ever thought about was myself. I was ready to start a new life and I was ecstatic. I had escaped our old world; my mission was complete. But you two are living a continuation of who you were back on Earth.

Watching you two really lit up my world. Despite your worries and fears, you had one, pure motivation: to get used to life in this world. I had escaped my old shackles and had a chance to walk a new path in life. Watching you two try your best inspired me to start something new.

Kazuki-kun is worried about the upcoming battle. Though he may feel uncertain, I can tell that he's trying to find his place in the world. As someone who knew who you were back on Earth, I think your efforts are nothing short of inspiring. It's hard to change who you are—believe me, I know—so watching you do this is simply incredible.

Usato-kun, you're an interesting fellow.

You act kind of stoic around me but deep down I know that you're incredibly strong-willed. Come to think of it, out of you, me, and Kazuki-kun, you were the first one to decide which path you would take in this world.

To be honest, I was really nervous when we talked in the forest. But not only were you unfazed by what I said, you sympathized with me and told me that you admire fantasy worlds.

When you told me that you accepted who I wanted to be, that was the happiest moment of all. I wasn't the fake Suzune Inukami I was back on Earth; I was the real me, in this world, and you accepted me for all that I am.

This might be a little too direct, but of all the people to get dragged to this world, I'm glad it was you. As much as you might deny it, you're irreplaceable to Kazuki-kun, and of course, to me as well.

That's why I'll do my best to be just like you.

When I made that promise to you in the forest, I wasn't kidding. I want to fight for the place where I—where we—all belong.

Both of you are here in this world.

I won't despair anymore.

—Suzune Inukami

Kazuki

▲ School Uniform   ▲ Informal wear   ▲ Armor

Blurin

Rose

▲ Team uniform

Usato

▲ School uniform ▲ Training uniform ▲ Team uniform

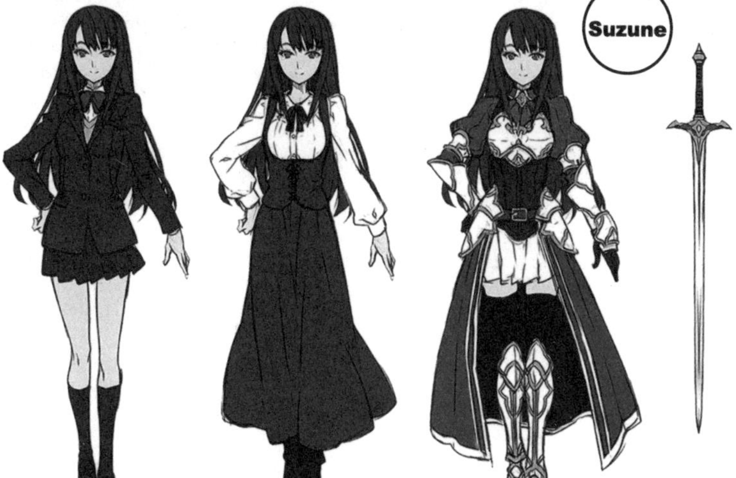

Suzune

▲ School uniform ▲ Informal wear ▲ Armor

Character Design

The Wrong Way to Use Healing Magic Volume 1
(CHIYUMAHO NO MACHIGATTA TSUKAIKATA -SENJO O KAKERU
KAIHUKUYOIN- Vol. 1)
©KUROKATA 2016
First published in Japan in 2016 by KADOKAWA CORPORATION, Tokyo.
English translation rights arranged with KADOKAWA CORPORATION, Tokyo.

ISBN: 978-1-64273-200-9

Written by KUROKATA
Art by KeG
Translated by Kristi Fernandez
English Edition Published by One Peace Books 2022

Printed in Canada
1 2 3 4 5 6 7 8 9 10

One Peace Books
43-32 22nd Street STE 204 Long Island City New York 11101
www.onepeacebooks.com